Broken and Bleeding Hearts

By E. A. Snively

Copyright

Publication date: December 2023

This novel is entirely a work of fiction. The names, characters and incidents portrayed in it are the work of the author's imagination. Any resemblance to actual persons, living or dead, events or localities is entirely coincidental.

Dedicated to Amazon Kindle Vella and my readers – thank you

Table of Contents

Chapter One: Meet Patrick

July 5, 2022

I'm free. Patrick exits the Secretary of State office, freedom firmly and FINALLY in his hands. *I'm free.* He stops at the door of his truck, clutching the handle with white-knuckled fingers, until he steadies his breathing.

It's ten in the morning – he has been in there an hour. It took them forever to get through everything. He knew his rights and was exercising them, but still, he knew someone would be watching him. Just because he was a "new man" didn't mean the old one was dead or even forgotten. He was in their books, but now he feels free. Well, technically. He still must find *her.* And all he has is a picture, name, and address…from twenty-five years ago. Still, it's the best he has. Once he finds her, apologizes, and hopefully doesn't get something thrown at him, he hopes he can finally begin a new life.

A new life at forty-five…what are the odds? He thinks about this as he drives out of the parking lot and heads to the diner to meet his friend. The last ten years he has tried to shadow his way back into the world. He didn't want to draw attention to himself, but he was starving for attention. Before the incident, he was a wild man. He had not cared much for school, barely graduating high school. He had hung around instead of going to college, because he had not known what he wanted, besides to party, and his grades would not have gotten him in to any schools. He loved going to parties, hooking up with all the pretty girls, getting drunk and high, hanging out with friends doing stupid sh…stuff.

Watch it, he thinks to himself. *Remember, you're not the same guy anymore. You're a good guy, trying to live a clean life, and you don't swear.*

Swearing was the hardest habit to break. Before the ten years of parole, the previous fifteen years had seen him behind bars. Do you think swearing is bad on the streets? Think again! It was nearly impossible to go a minute without hearing someone swear. Swearing was one of the only freedoms they still had in prison. He had pleaded not guilty, and his penalty wasn't as steep as it could have been, but still…FIFTEEN years in JAIL?!? And during his prime!?! *Stop that*, he chides himself. *You're a changed man now. Remember Pastor Ted. You took a life and you paid for it.*

Pastor Ted was the prison minister where Patrick served his time. While Patrick went in a wild, uncouth youth, Pastor Ted saw his potential. He pushed past Patrick's cussing him out and started asking him questions when he noticed Patrick trying to appear like he wasn't listening to the sermon. Of course, Patrick had tried to shrug Pastor Ted's attempts off, but Pastor Ted was persistent – for which Patrick was eternally grateful. Patrick had felt abandoned. No one had visited him after the accident. And that's what it was – an accident. He didn't mean to kill anyone. He wasn't over the limit that much. He had no ill intentions.

Stop that, Patrick scolds himself again. *It's what it's, no use trying to fix that past.* Patrick is not that sad to let go of his family. Honestly, he's probably better off without them. His parents were in and out of jail themselves. He has four younger siblings, but he was never that close to any of them. Honestly, his parents were probably thrilled not to have to worry about one more mouth to feed. No money going towards him meant it could go towards meth and other drugs. Patrick *did* wonder if he should try to find his siblings and see what had become of them…but none of them had tried to contact him and no one ever visited. They clearly had not cared about him then, so why should he care about them now?

Stop feeling sorry for yourself, Patrick sighs inwardly. *They left you and you would have a harder time living straight if you tried to find them and get back with any of them. And you're going to live a straight life now*, he says to himself as he passes a liquor store. Shaking his head, he continues his way to the diner.

Chapter Two: Meet Mickie

Mickie sits in her armchair, drinking water and petting her cat, Sebastian, when she hears Karen's ringtone.

"I'm a Barbie girl in a Barbie worrlldd"

"Hey, Karen," Mickie says, picking up her phone.

"Come on, Mickie. Stop moping. Come grab drinks with me!" Karen demands over the phone.

"No, I'm good," Mickie sighs.

"You can't swear off drinking forever. People will think you're a prude!" Karen warns.

"What people?" Mickie laughs.

"The people you're gonna meet tonight," Karen pushes.

"I told you, I'm just gonna stay in tonight. Watch Netflix and chill and all that," Mickie walks across the living room to the kitchen to refill her water.

Karen pauses then quietly replies, "It's been twenty-five years. When was the last time you slept with a guy?"

Mickie almost spills her water. "KAREN!?!"

"What? You have needs and you keep yourself in this depressed state. At least primp and take a walk. For me?" Karen begs.

Mickie sighs in defeat, "OK."

"Great, I'll pick you up in half an hour," and Karen hangs up.

Mickie shakes her head and smiles – that's just like Karen. Well...she should at least put on her one dress that Karen doesn't hate and brush her hair...had she even showered or put on deodorant today? A quick whiff told her no. With a sigh she gets ready for a quick shower and even quicker wardrobe change (forget hair and makeup, she would just blow dry and put on concealer).

~~~~~~

Jacob: Hey mom

Mickie: Jacob! How are you?

Jacob: Good. You OK today?

Mickie: Yes, of course. I'm doing great. Getting ready to go out, actually.

Jacob: yeah? Where's Karen taking you this time?

Mickie: HAHAHA! How did you know?

Jacob: mom, you never go out by yourself

Mickie: THAT'S NOT TRUE!

Jacob: mom, don't use all caps unless you're mad. And yes, it's true.

Jacob: So, where's she taking you?

Mickie: IDK

Jacob: ...

Jacob: OK then. Try to have fun. Tell Karen I say hi

Mickie: Will do. Love you.

Jacob: love you too

Mickie: Tell Mara I say hi, as well.

Jacob: k

As soon as the last text comes through, Karen knocks on the door and lets herself in. "Come on! It's getting late, and we don't want to be around only drunks. You're wearing *that* again?"

Mickie sighs, "It's the only one you like."

Karen rolls her eyes and grumbles, "Then we need to go dress shopping soon."

Mickie just grabs her purse and slings it over her head and shoulder. "OK, Karen, where are we off to tonight?"

Karen looks at Mickie and shakes her head. "You're dressed like a middle-aged mom."

"I am a middle-aged mom," Mickie laughs.

"No....well, I guess, yes, but your son is out of the house. You should be dressing to impress, not dressing to show off pictures of your son - who is an adult now and no longer lives with you," Karen emphasizes.

Mickie sighs and hangs her head. "Look, Karen. It's hard enough without Jacob here. And on the anniversary – "

"No, you can't call it that anymore. Anniversaries have a joyous connotation - this is just an excuse to stay miserable, depressed, and alone your whole life," Karen interrupts.

Mickie fires up and retorts, "Well, at least I'm not a middle-aged, three-time divorcee!"

Karen and Mickie glare at each other as their words fill the air with tension and unspoken pain. "OK," Karen starts, "I'm sorry. You can call it an anniversary. And if you don't want to go anywhere fun today, I respect that."

"Thank you," begins Mickie.

"I'm not done," Karen cuts in. "You do keep yourself closed up and don't let any guys close enough to you to even see if you're ready for a new relationship. And keeping yourself cooped up in your little house with your cat - I mean, come on Mickie, you fit the sad single woman stereotype to a T. Let's at least go out, have a nice dinner, maybe see if any single guys are there who might pay for our meals, and then go look at new clothes for you."

Mickie can't help it; she laughs and walks to her best friend, giving her an apologetic hug.

Chapter Three: Mickie, Bar None

July 5, 2022, *Evening*

"When I said, 'It doesn't have to be a seedy bar,' I was still thinking bar...not bar and grill" Karen complains as they walk up the sidewalk to Applebee's.

Mickie just shakes her head and smiles slightly. She hasn't gone to a bar in almost twenty years, not since the last time she allowed Karen to take her to one. Never again. Mickie had a panic attack and the bouncer had dragged her out – just seconds after entering the bar; it was humiliating. It was also why she stood firm on her absolutely-no-bars rule (and Karen never really pushed that hard). Once they sit, *in the bar area*, Karen starts looking around for her next potential guy.

"What about those two guys?" She nods while taking a sip from her mixer. The guys in question were clearly drunk and hitting on the barista.

"No way," Mickie answers, taking a drink from her lemon water. Karen continues to survey the bar area, pointing out different guys in turn. Mickie, of course, declines all of them while Karen keeps coming back to two guys who she probably will make eye contact with after her second drink. Mickie is not interested in anyone here. And then *he* walks in the door.

"Table for one; no bar, thanks" Mickie hears him tell the host.

Mickie watches the host take him around the corner, and then, miraculously, just on the other side of her divider so she can still watch him.

"Mickie, you're not paying attention to me! I said which one should I go to first? Blue Shirt looks like he may leave soon, but Collar Guy is closer in age and not so drunk. Neither of them interested you, I know, but –"

"Have you ever seen him before?" Mickie interrupts, using her cup to show No Bar guy. Karen got out way more than Mickie and paid more attention to the male population.

"Ooh...who?!?" Karen squeals, accidentally spilling a little of her third drink on the table (never herself – she wasn't a sloppy drunk) as she leans forward to see. "Yum!" She approves, then quizzically looks at Mickie. "Have you been drinking some of my mixers?"

"What?!?! No! Of course not. You know I don't drink," Mickie retorts.

"Then why are you asking me about a man?" Karen demands.

Mickie sighs and looks back at him. "I don't know. There is just something about him. I felt attracted to him as soon as he walked in. And not like *physically*, but like a magnet. I literally looked up as he walked in and wasn't able to take my eyes off him. Have you ever seen him around?" she asks again, but Karen is already turning the corner.

"Karen!" Mickie squeaks, but Karen either can't hear or is choosing to ignore her. Mickie leans farther across the table to hopefully hear the whole conversation.

"Hey," Karen starts.

No Bar looks up at her and raises an eyebrow, "Hey?"

"Care to join me and my friend over there?" She points towards the bar area. A flicker passes over his face, and he shakes his head while politely trying to decline, "No, thanks." Karen hesitates a moment then notices his Pepsi; she smiles and adds, "My friend doesn't drink either. And she would really like to meet you." Mickie groans and slouches back in her seat, but not taking her eyes off No Bar and Karen.

No Bar looks over to where Karen is pointing and sees Mickie. He appraises the situation and then smiles at Karen. "Sure," he says, as he tells his waiter he will be moving to our table. "Does your friend have a name?" Mickie groans again and shrinks farther into the booth, then notices it makes a weird crease around her breasts and sits back upright as they turn the corner. Mickie stands to introduce herself, or at least tries to. She bumps into the table as she stands up and knocks her water over as she tries to balance herself. Mickie, horrified, glances up quickly to see No Bar grab the napkins to catch the water before it drips on the floor.

"I swear I haven't had anything to drink" Mickie blurts out, remembering how he seemed very against drinking.

No Bar smiles and replies, "Accidents happen, no worries." And sits down across from Mickie, following Karen into the booth.

Mickie feels like she's in high school again. Her body is acting like it'sn't acted in an exceptionally long time; she's extremely uncomfortable with how awkward she feels and how she seems to get weak at the knees when he smiles.

Karen watches all of this like a prime-time movie and starts the introductions. "I'm Karen, by the way. And this is my friend, Mickie." She looks at him as a way of introduction.

"I'm Paul."

Chapter Four: Patrick's Self Talk

Patrick stares at the short information:

Michelle A Brenner

5441 Leland Road

Hadad, MI 48055

Her picture was of an eighteen-year-old girl, just graduated from Hadad High School, and just married to Benjamin Brenner. She had long, wavy, blonde hair; light blue eyes; was slender looking; an easy-going smile with slightly parted teeth; a little heavy on the makeup *(though it was the late 1990s)*. Patrick sighs. Michelle would be forty-three now, probably. Did blondes go gray or white? What if she dyed her hair? Would she be wearing glasses by now? He himself wore readers, when necessary. What if she had let herself go since the accident? What if she had moved or changed her name? *What if she had died?*

These thoughts plague Patrick. He has a steady job now – working hard while on parole to move up the factory ladder. He had saved up his money to regain his license and buy a used truck; then he had saved frugally, so once he finished parole, he could move and rent a cheap apartment. Pastor Ted baptized him fifteen years ago. Patrick still helped at the nonprofit Second Chances thrift store. He's ready to fully move past this accident.

He turns to his own folder, pulling his paperwork out. Flipping it open, he sees his picture: twenty-years-old, scowling, high forehead, sallow cheeks, puffed out bottom lip, mahogany brown eyes. Now he's forty-five; more stoic than scowling mostly, but rarely smiling; has a jailbird look to him – rough, muscular, underfed; widow's peak hairline. He has changed but maybe it was more inward than outward. He still lives in Michigan; more mature-looking than his twenty-year-old self than anything else. His hair is slightly longer now, but that's only because short hair is too much of a reminder of his prison years.

Patrick sighs. There is no point holding it off. He had made his way to Hadad, rented an apartment, gotten his truck – nothing left but to seek Michelle A. Brenner out. He would have left last night after dinner, but two women sidetracked him. Patrick slowly smiles to himself. Last night was fun. He had gone out to eat after filling out paperwork with his new name all day. He had Michelle's paper with him and was going to visit the house afterwards – best to just get it done; like ripping off a Band-Aid. Now that he thought about it, maybe it was God intervening. What had he been thinking, going to visit on the anniversary of her husband's death? That could have gone horribly wrong. *Like a nightmare.*

So, God intervened. He had just ordered his Diet Pepsi when a woman had asked him to join her group. In the past, he would have been part of a group. Now he was a loner. And he's fine with that. He's better off on his own; much better at controlling situations by himself. But last night...it was like something else was controlling the situation, but in a safe way. He had no idea why he said yes, or why he had been like his charming, old self. He had not been like that in a very long time.

He used to be a charmer. He had been in high school, as a young man before the accident, even a handful of times that first year on probation. He was always careful, but sex was fun and pleasurable. Then he told Pastor Ted about it one time over their breakfast meetups and Pastor Ted had told him that sex wasn't something that was supposed to be done whenever the urge hit. Sex was meant for marriage.

Patrick respected Pastor Ted but giving up sex was hard! And... it's not like many women would want to marry him once they learned about his past. Plus, you know, the whole being forty-five thing...it's not like he's young anymore. The women he would end up dating would probably have kids, and even grown kids wasn't something on his radar. He had enough complicated family baggage to not want anyone else's.

So, he had not invited either of the girls over last night, but it had been a pleasurable time. He had flirted and charmed, allowed the one lady to touch his leg and arm. But the other lady...there was something about her. He hoped they would meet again sometime. Of course, there had been the exchange of numbers...but he didn't plan on calling. He enjoyed himself, but that was scary, not being in control of himself or the situation. Better to just remember it as a relaxing evening and move on.

Move on to Michelle A Brenner.

Chapter Five: Mickie is Michelle!

Karen: Has he called you?

Mickie: No.

Karen: Me neither. I wonder how come?!?!

Mickie: I know. You were giving him all the right signals.

Karen: Dear, he was into YOU!

Mickie: WHAT?!?

Karen: Oh, come on, it was obvious he was more into you than me. I was just having fun flirting - just in case he changed his mind.

Mickie: Changed his mind?

Karen: If that man wasn't a charmer, then I don't know my men anymore.

Mickie: If he were a charmer, then why would he sit with us? Why wouldn't he drink any alcohol? I think you're wrong.

Karen: YOU LIKE HIM!!!!!!

Mickie: WHAT?????

Karen: You're defending him! You spent two hours with him, and you're smitten!

Karen: He has to call you.

Karen: Or I'll hunt him down.

Karen: We're going to Applebee's every night until he comes back.

Mickie: Slow down!

Karen: ...

Mickie: I still can't believe you gave him my number.

Karen: Oh, come on. You can't still be upset over that.

Mickie: You didn't even ask me!

Karen: Come on. You're only acting this way because you like him, and you're upset he hasn't called yet.

Mickie's doorbell rings. *Saved by the bell,* she thinks to herself and then smirks, remembering the TV show.

Mickie: Doorbell. TTYL.

Karen: Maybe it's Paul!!!!

Mickie rolls her eyes and chuckles. Karen gave Paul her number, not her address. Then Mickie's smile dips back down. *Why didn't he call?* She would never admit it to Karen, but she was glad Karen gave him her number. There was something about Paul that she had never felt with anyone else before. It was like a strange pull. The doorbell rings again just as Mickie is within reach. "I'm coming," she calls through the door and then unlocks it, turns the knob, and opens it.

"Paul!"

He looks at her and she at once can tell he had no idea he was ringing her doorbell. His mouth falls open and then she swears she sees him do some quick calculations before smiling.

"Hey...Mickie," he says, only somewhat strained.

"Paul! What are you doing here?" Mickie stammers, thinking to herself, *"How did he find my address? Is he stalking me? DID Karen give him my address?!?"*

Paul hesitates for a moment, still working through that mental puzzle before he answers, "Wow! Such a strange coincidence! You're on my route." Then he slightly grimaces before plastering the smile back in place.

"I don't understand," Mickie responds, still very confused. "What route? You're not wearing a uniform or have any materials with you." She's starting to think maybe she should just close the door and call the police. *Where had she put her cellphone?*

Paul's shoulders sag a little. "I'm sorry for startling you, Mickie." Then he hesitates and adds, "And I'm sorry for not calling you - that was a dick move on my part." Then he realizes he may have said something uncouth and scrambles to apologize. "I meant; I should have called. I'm sorry. And this has absolutely nothing to do with Applebee's! I'm part of a lawn maintenance company, and I'm out canvassing today, looking for new customers. It just really threw me off when you opened the door. That's why I seemed so cagey. I'm sorry." He smiles sheepishly at her.

Mickie thinks about this for a moment and then shrugs. Window companies had stopped by her house before and they didn't wear any certain outfits...made sense if he were canvassing, he would just look hot in jeans and a dress shirt, unbuttoned at the top...*WAIT! Answer him! Don't mentally undress him!* "Oh...yeah, that makes sense. And, yes, it's fine. It's not like I was waiting by the phone or anything. I didn't even know Karen was going to give you my number. She'll get a hoot once she hears about this." *Hoot? Really?* Mickie was inwardly groaning at her own patheticness.

"Well," Paul begins again.

"OH! Right! Lawn maintenance!" Mickie interrupts. She looks around her yard and notices the weedy, overgrown flower beds and bare lawn. "I, uh, don't have too much work, but I'd be happy to set up a time to have you come by and do whatever it's you do." Then Mickie stops and blushes. "I mean, I guess it may not be you. And I may not need to be around – "

Paul interrupts her. "Mickie, calm down. It's all good. I'll have a look around and when my partner is done looking at the house down the street, I'll have him come over here and we'll talk about options with you."

Mickie looks like she's ready to blush herself into a heat stroke but stammers out a squeaky "OK," before stepping back inside and closing the door. She leans against it a moment, then runs to her phone.

Mickie: You won't believe it over text. Call.

Chapter Six: Patrick's Lawn Service

A string of swear words runs through Patrick's mind as he tries processing everything. He knows he should not swear - and he's working on it - but even Pastor Ted would understand at a time like this. Hopefully, God would forgive him once he figures things out. Patrick pulls out his phone to call Tom.

"Pick up. Pick up. Pick up. Pick up." Patrick mutters to himself, walking around the house, seemingly inspecting the landscape.

"Hello," says a slow drawl. *Oh, thank goodness.*

"Tom! Tom, I need you to come to this address I'm texting you. RIGHT NOW! Come dressed as a landscaper!" Patrick whisper yells into his phone, looking to make sure Mickie is not watching him.

"Whoa, slow down there, bud. What's up?" Tom's lazy voice hitches enough that Patrick knows he has stood up.

"So, you know that girl from the accident? The one that I want to try to make things right with? Turns out she's the same woman I ate dinner with two nights ago!" Patrick's voice is urgent, with a harshness to it that Tom doesn't usually hear.

"Does she know it's you?" Patrick hears him dressing and tries to slow his racing heart and mind.

"I mean, she knows it's me from the other night, but she doesn't know that I'm the Patrick from her past!"

"How did you manage that? I'm leaving now, by the way."

"Good. And because it's been twenty-five years – people change. And I may have introduced myself as Paul at the restaurant." Patrick paces back and forth. There is not much to

Mickie's landscaping: one tree, two weedy patches that look like they were tries at flower beds years ago, and patchy grass.

"What? Oh, right...the name change. Why would you introduce yourself to two strangers by your new name?" Patrick hears Tom's turn signal.

"I'm in the town where the accident happened. I want a fresh start, and I didn't want them to be connected in any way to the accident or Michelle. I obviously had no CLUE that Mickie would be short for Michelle and DEFINITELY not the SAME MICHELLE!" Patrick leans against one of the trees. How stupid to think there was a connection between them. God sure had a sick sense of humor. The phone call ended.

"Hey, Paul." Tom saunters over to the front walk. Patrick turns and walks toward him, trying to force an easy grin in case Mickie is watching.

"Hey, so I told the lady inside that I'm canvassing new lawns for our landscape and lawn care services. I told her that once you got here, we'd go over our packages with her." Patrick tells Tom, showing him the measly front and side yard. "Here, let me show you the backyard as well." And Patrick gestures to the back of the house. Tom raises an eyebrow at him but continues the charade, walking beside him.

"Really? That was the best lie you could produce on the spot?" Tom barely whispers out the side of his mouth.

"I panicked, OK? What am I going to do?" Patrick is sweating and Tom claps him on the back.

"Don't worry. We'll do what men do well: lie our butts off and hope she doesn't catch on." Tom smiles at his own joke but Patrick frowns. "What is it, Pat, I mean Paul?" Tom asks, noticing the frown.

"I don't know. I don't want to keep lying to this woman. But I don't want to make my apology like this, either." Patrick mumbles, trying to work through his own emotions. Something else nags at him.

"You like this woman, don't you, Pa-Paul?!? You can't go liking her!" Tom lets loose a quick volley of swear words under his breath.

"Keep your voice down, please!" Patrick begs, but Tom is walking up the front steps. "What are you doing?!?!?" Patrick hisses.

"Paul, get in the truck." Tom commands, just as Mickie opens the front door. "Ma'am, good day. I'm sorry to hear that there has been a misunderstanding. Unfortunately, since you and Paul have a history, however slight, I can't allow him to work on your lawn. I'll send another guy over soon. Good day, ma'am." And with that, Tom turns and walks briskly to the truck.

Patrick looks out the passenger window at Mickie and they lock eyes. She looks shocked and concerned. He instinctively raises his hands in a farewell gesture.

"Put that hand down, you look like a fool." Tom huffs as he turns the key in the ignition.

"Where are we going? My truck's parked down the block – " but Tom cuts him off.

"Coffee." Tom barks. Then he shifts his gaze over to Patrick, adding, "I want the whole story."

Chapter Seven: Patrick Brews a Story

"You like her?!?" Tom hasn't been able to get off this one point. Usually, he's more helpful than a broken record, but not today.

"I don't know if like is the best word. More like attracted. Literally. I feel pulled to her." Patrick finishes his first cup of black coffee and flags down the server to get a refill.

"OK....OK. I hear you. But don't you think that she may hate your very existence? No, no... PATRICK'S very existence?!?" The server refills both cups of coffee and Tom asks her to just bring a pot over and leave it.

"Yes..." Patrick responds slowly, "But I'm PAUL."

"Dude, I don't care if you say your name is Santa Claus, you're Patrick Lawrence and there's no running away from it!" Tom's face is turning the color of grape juice, barely able to control his incredulity and frustration.

Patrick sighs and leans back against the chair. He knows Tom is right. If Mickie knew he was the one who killed her high school sweetheart husband, she would want nothing to do with him. But there was still this magnetic attraction he felt...and he was sure she felt it too. If they could explore that connection, maybe she would not hate him.

"Earth to Patrick," Tom cuts into Patrick's wondering. "You were thinking about a way around this, right?"

"Yeah. And I think I'm going to ask her out," Patrick decides.

Tom swears adamantly. "OK, man, listen to me. There is no 'if she finds out.' She will! That's how these things go. And trust me, you will be in a worse place than you have been these past ten years. She may do you the honors of killing you, just to make sure you and all your aliases never bother her again."

"I disagree. Here is why. I feel a strange pull towards her, right? I would bet my truck that she feels the same way. Look, I don't know if it's soul mate crap, God being merciful, or even her dead husband wanting us both to be able to move past this, but something strong is at work. I must figure out what it's. I need to spend more time with her. Then, when it's the right time, after I have figured everything out, I'll tell her the truth. I'll tell her who I really am, apologize for not telling her sooner, and maybe we'll have connected deeply enough that she will be able to forgive me. But I can't very well tell her who I am now – she would never let me get close to her. And I need to figure out why there is this pull!" Patrick throws himself back against the booth.

Tom listens to and watches his friend. He had never seen Patrick this way before. He didn't know him when the accident happened, so he doesn't know if this is old Patrick coming through, but he feels for his friend. "Is there any way she may remember it's you? Have you two ever seen each other?"

"Yes," Patrick replies, his eyes closed. "At the court hearing, right after the accident." Patrick replays everything in his mind. It was the middle of the night, right after the fourth of July. He and some friends had snuck out to a deserted, private, lakefront property after the fireworks show to drink beer. They were always doing crazy, stupid stuff like that. Breaking rules just for the high. He and a girl...he could not even remember her name now, they had not met before that night and she had never contacted him after, had snuck off to have sex. When they had come back, one of the guys sprayed them with beer and began teasing them. Patrick had stormed off to his truck and left them, knowing he would pay hell because of making one of the family vehicles smell of beer. He was blasting Sean Combs when the headlights appeared out of nowhere. At the court hearing, he heard how he had forgotten to turn on his high beams in his anger and was partly over the line going over a hill. His truck had just crested, had more power behind it, and was bigger, so he and the little car crashed and went down the hill, his truck crushing the car between it and a pole. The other driver was ruled dead at the scene. Patrick's alcohol level was also a little over the limit (not much, but enough to be a DUI). It was an easy, open and shut case: he could not pay for an experienced defense lawyer, so the judge charged him with Vehicular Manslaughter and fifteen years in jail. Mickie had been there, as the dead boy's wife, but was completely beside herself. It was the parents who looked at him with hate in their eyes.

"Yes, she was at the court hearing, but I don't think she ever looked at me. She was pretty shaken up." Patrick opens his eyes to see Tom watching him intently. "Look, I know it's completely insane, but I have to do this."

Tom raises his mug in a toast, "here's to you figuring out that feeling…and her not killing you." Patrick raises his mug and clinks it against Tom's, feeling as if something big is about to go down.

Chapter Eight: Mickie Gets Advice

Karen gently rocks on the recliner while drinking her Diet. She had come straight over to Mickie's from work, bringing dinner and drinks when Mickie had texted she had even more developments on the Paul front. For the first time in her life, Mickie was *finally* supplying the juicy stories. "So," Karen says, as she takes another drink, "what news on Paul?"

"He came back over yesterday," Mickie blurts out.

"Really?" This brings Karen's rocking to a halt as she leans forward. "What did he say?"

"He..." Mickie begins, then pauses to blush. The truth of it's that Mickie could still scarcely believe what had happened. Yesterday, after Paul's boss picked him up and said he would not be able to do her lawn care because they knew each other, he had waved goodbye before leaving. That in and of itself was strange, but the wave...there just seemed to be something strange between them. She had left a voicemail for Karen before she started pacing, trying to figure out why she felt like something was up. Karen called during her lunch break and agreed it seemed odd that the boss had driven him away, but maybe they were worried about some kind of liability issue. Then....then, an hour after she got off the phone with Karen, her doorbell rang, and *again* it was Paul!

"Hey," he said, and he brought a bouquet of flowers from behind his back. "I hope I didn't startle you earlier. And I hope my boss didn't give you too hard a time. I'm sorry I can't work on your lawn, but I was wondering if you would be interested in going out with me on Saturday?"

It was so sweet and romantic. Mickie had taken the bouquet, breathed in the fragrance, then replied, "I'd love to. What time and where?" *What had she been thinking?!? She had not gone out on a date by herself in years!!!*

"I was thinking maybe dinner at Barb's diner in town. It's a little homey, but the food can't be beaten," he had responded, smiling at her.

"Sure, I'll meet you there about five?" Mickie had asked, still unsure where this suave person speaking from inside her had come from.

"Actually, can it be about seven? I work tomorrow and then I would like to freshen up before seeing you," Paul had replied. *Did he ever stop smiling?*

At this, Mickie blushed. *Five*?!? What was she, sixty?!? And he wanted to look nice for her and she had *nothing* to wear for a date. Especially not for someone as fine-looking as Paul...oh...she needed to shave. She needed to answer him!!! "Oh, um, yeah, absolutely." Well, Miss Suave had disappeared.

Mickie replays all of this to Karen who starts laughing. "Oh, Mickie, CONGRATULATIONS! You're finally back in the game!" Karen yells, still chuckling.

"I don't see what's so funny. I make a complete fool of myself around him. And how do I know I'm ready to be back in the game?" Mickie glares at Karen, but then adds. "Karen, please, I'm so confused and nervous. I need help."

"Girl, you need LOTS of help." Karen states matter-of-factly. "OK, first, you agreed to a date, so you're back in the game and ready. Let go of that little ball of guilt. Ben would have wanted you to move on long before this. Jacob wants you to move on. You're the only one holding yourself back. It's been twenty-five years since Ben died. You raised Jacob on your own as a good, single, hardworking mother. You put your son above everything. But he's on his own now. He would probably feel better if he knew you were finally taking care of your needs. And honey, you haven't been happy since Ben died. You deserve a sweet romance. And whatever strange pull you and Pauly boy have on each other - it's mutual and strong. So, let's get up and check out your clothes."

Karen leads the way into Mickie's bedroom and goes to her closet. It doesn't take long to rifle through everything in there. "OK, there is nothing worth wearing for any occasion in here," Karen says bluntly.

"Hey, my black dress is in there!" Mickie replies, defensively.

"Yes, and Paul already saw you in it and you don't want him thinking you only have two pairs of clothes," Karen retorts, now looking through Mickie's dresser. "WHOA! I didn't know you had thongs!?!" Karen exclaims, turning around holding a tiny, lacy thong.

Mickie blushes. "It was from one of the wedding showers.... I forgot I still had those. They must be shoved way in the back because I haven't worn them since...." Mickie stops and blushes again; luckily, Karen has already turned around and pulls out her tighter pair of jeans and a floral pattern top.

"OK," Karen begins, turning around and surveying the outfit she put together. She goes back to the closet and pulls out the black heals Mickie wears with her black dress. "Finished." On the bed, besides the jeans, top, and heels, are a push-up bra and the lacy thong.

"Karen..." Mickie begins, but Karen cuts her off.

"Look, you're going to a diner, so you don't need to wear a dress. But wearing a flattering outfit and underwear that accentuates your butt and boobs will go a long way, trust me. Before your next date, we need to go shopping. Now, let's start on your hair and makeup!" Karen is almost giddy in anticipation, but Mickie can't take her eyes off the thong and wonders if she can even still pull off wearing them.

Chapter Nine: First Date

Mickie and Paul sit at a little square table for two at Barb's Diner. Paul stands when she walks in, then realizes he doesn't know what he should do. Mickie smiles nervously then puts out her hand for a handshake. They quickly shake hands then both sit down. Their server comes over and both order a Diet.

"Hi," "So," they say at the same time. They smile at each other.

"Go on; you first," Paul says.

"Hi," Mickie repeats, then blushes. "Um, this is nice. Thanks for inviting me out." Her blush creeps down her neck and she takes a long drink of her Diet.

"Well," Paul begins, then takes a deep breath and plunges straight in, "I just feel this sort of connection between us."

"Oh my gosh! Me too!" Mickie gasps, setting her Diet down and leaning forward. "Do you have any reason why? Have we met before?"

Paul barely even hesitates, "I don't think that's it, or we would have recognized each other. Maybe we should get to know each other a little better. Tell me about yourself; besides the fact that we keep running into each other and feel this strange connection." He smiles, picking up his own Diet to drink from while she talks.

Mickie blushes again but begins, "Well, I don't really have that much to tell. I grew up here. I'm an only child. Both of my parents are dead. I was married right out of high school to my high school sweetheart. He died in a car crash shortly after our wedding. I found out I was pregnant pretty soon after. So, I have a son, Jacob, who is the light of my life. He lives about forty-five minutes away, is in a committed relationship, and I'm expecting him to pop the question to her any time now. I never remarried; I worked as a waitress and housekeeper to make ends meet for us. I wrote a book that did decently well, in its time. Once my son started working and demanded to help with bills, I started writing again; I hope to make my living as a writer, but currently still work as a waitress." She takes a drink and they both order burgers, fries, and refills.

"Wow! A writer! That's cool! What do you write?" Paul asks, leaning forward, and pulling out his phone.

"Oh, lots of things. That first book was called Heavyhearted and started out more like a memoir but written as a fiction book; it ended with a romantic happily ever after with a new relationship," Mickie replies, then quickly adds, "Which never happened for me in real life, but it sure upset Ben's parents. They wrote us off after that. They thought I had already moved on, was secretly seeing someone, and that Jacob was the result of sleeping with someone else. It was crazy, but they were never the same after Ben's accident."

"That's awful!" Paul exclaims. "They should have known how much you were hurting and that you were just writing a wonderful daydream." He breathes heavily, clearly upset.

"How would you know?" Mickie asks.

"Because I can tell by the way you described yourself. Did you have any serious relationships after Ben?" Paul questions.

"I haven't really had anything serious, but I have been on dates over the years. You remember Karen, right? She sets me up every now and then," Mickie answers.

Paul smiles, remembering Karen at Applebee's. "So, any reason why you never remarried? Please tell me it's not because of your idiot in-laws?"

Mickie smiles, appreciative of the protection in his voice on her behalf. "They're not idiots, and no, not because of them." Mickie stops smiling and frowns, and Paul can hear a little quiver in her voice as she continues. "Honestly, it's because of me. I'm so vanilla."

"Vanilla?" Paul asks, clearly confused.

"Plain. You know those 'Never Have I Ever' things on Facebook?" Mickie quickly asks. Paul shakes his head no. "Oh," Mickie replies, then continues, "Well, they say something along the lines of 'Give yourself one point for each thing you've done and then comment the number at the bottom' and I always have one of the lowest scores." Paul still looks confused, so Mickie pulls out her phone and finds one, then shows it to him. "See? Things like dying your hair - well, that's a bad first one because I do dye my roots now." She stops for a moment, realizing what she said and blushes, then laughs. "Oh, Karen is going to die of embarrassment when I tell her about this date. Anyways, I have never shot a gun, never been in a hot air balloon, never been on TV, never met anyone famous, never sang karaoke - like in a bar, I figured in a machine at home doesn't count - never been in a limo, never – " Mickie blushes again.

Paul notices the blush and finishes, "Never been skinny dipping?" Mickie blushes all the way down her neck and Paul smiles which leads to light chuckles, then goes back to the list. "Given birth? Yes, Jacob," Paul answers himself. "Skipped school?" he asks, and Mickie shakes her head no. "Really? Man, I skipped more than I went," he chuckles again. "Gotten a tattoo? Man, these are great first date questions!" Mickie shakes her head no, again. They continue through the list for Mickie and then go through with Paul answering them.

"Where's your tattoo?" Mickie asks, and Paul shows her his right shoulder tattoo of a phoenix rising from a fire. "It's gorgeous," Mickie breathes, wanting to touch it but not wanting to cross any boundaries. Mickie blushes when Paul admits he has been skinny dipping but doesn't question him about that one. "See? You have a higher number than me." Then she bows her head and adds quietly, "I think that's why no one goes on many dates with me. I'm not someone to just do one-night stands. I don't have anything risqué or do anything risky. I'm just...plain. And guys expect me to be loose since I got married at eighteen and had a child at nineteen. And when they find out I'm not, they think I'm boring." Mickie lowers her head as her eyes fill.

Paul reaches over, puts one hand on top of hers, then raises his other hand to her chin and lifts her head up. "I don't think you're boring," he whispers, then adds, "And I'd like to take you out on another date, if you're willing."

Chapter Ten: Patrick Can Make Her Dreams Come True

Patrick lay on his couch, reflecting on the evening. It had been his first date with Mickie. He says first because they already agreed to meet next week for another date. He still can't believe he's dating the woman whose life he wrecked twenty-five years ago. He knows Tom is right, and that this whole venture is crazy because eventually she will find out *(it always works out that way)*, but he can't help himself. Besides the crazy pull he described to Tom, he's very attracted to this woman. He smiles to himself as he recalls the evening.

He had gotten there early so he could have a table ready for them. He had not wanted to pick a fancy restaurant, because he wasn't sure if they were dating or just going out to get to know one another better. He figured the diner was a good spot, since everyone loved the home cooked meals and cozy atmosphere; he also figured that would put less pressure on them since he didn't know what she thought this meeting would be. When she came in wearing those hip hugging jeans and black heels though, he was very aware of where he wanted them to be. The top being decently form-fitting and showing a hint of cleavage made him suspect she may want this to be a date as well. Of course, she didn't have the confidence of her friend, Karen. That first awkward moment really threw him off his game, but luckily, she helped them navigate through it.

He was glad she ordered a hamburger and fries – he felt it showed confidence and less awkwardness. She wasn't afraid to get a little messy and show she liked more than salads; maybe that was a benefit of dating in your forties. Then she started talking about that Never Have I Ever photo. She was honest about dying her roots, which he saw as another vote of confidence, but then she had blushed and laughed saying she had not meant to share that little beauty secret with him. Maybe she felt comfortable enough around him to let that slip, but he thought it more likely she just wasn't the type to keep secrets. Going through the list though, she really had not done risky things in her life.

Suddenly, Patrick sits bolt upright. He pulls out his phone and types in Never Have I Ever to the search engine and then clicks on Images. He finds the one he thinks she had pulled up and starts reading the list again. Forget the fact that he has done more things than her on the list. He suddenly has a crazy idea; he can make all her dreams come true. Well, maybe not that dramatic, but he can help her feel less – what was the word she used again – vanilla. He opens another tab and starts looking for shooting ranges. There is one in town, but they don't open until tomorrow. *OK.* He searches for paper and settles on the back of an envelope. *Next.* He's not going to do anything to put her in danger, like getting a ticket. Skipping school may be a little difficult, considering she's not in school, and she didn't even have a normal office job to skip - he would have to think about that one some more. He scans the list for the easily possible options.

He has a great idea for meeting someone famous, and maybe for even getting on TV; he buys four tickets, thinking it might put less pressure on them if they bring along Tom and Karen. It's definitely risky contacting several tattoo artists to see when their next opening will be – he didn't know how he would pull that one off, but he also knew it would be several weeks out, so if the first few didn't go over well, he could always cancel the tattoo session. After spending an hour and a half looking stuff up and producing ideas to help Mickie cross things off her Never Have I Ever list, he finally calls it a night. It was midnight. He had had a busy day at work, an exciting first date, and an even more exciting time planning the next several weeks' worth of dates for them. He figures he will surprise her with the first one, hopefully the shooting range, just because he feels that would be the least nerve-wracking item for her to cross off. If they were not able to fit them in next week, he would have to go to one of his backups that didn't require reservations but would require a little more courage from her.

He's incredibly happy as he undresses for the night. It feels good to be doing something for someone. He realizes that right now it's not out of a love interest but rather wanting to help her out as a friend; however, he's also acutely aware of how his gaze had kept wandering to the hint of cleavage and how he had loved watching her walk out of the restaurant *(man, she had a very nice ass...et)*. He smiles as he rolls onto his side; it's been quite a long time since he has looked forward to anything fun.

Chapter Eleven: Mickie and the Shooting Range

Mickie looks at her reflection, wondering where Paul plans to go today. He had told her to dress casually and wear tennis shoes. Personally, she was more comfortable in tennis shoes, but thought that was a strange request. Were they going to do something sporty? She guessed he might be a sports guy – he was buff enough – but he didn't seem like the kind of guy who would take his date to go play basketball or something. Either way, she thought she looked all right: she was wearing tennis shoes, jeans, and a Michael Jackson T-shirt.

Ding, dong!

Mickie answers the door and sees Paul dressed like herself: tennis shoes, jeans, and a T-shirt. He smiles at her, his smile broadening as he notices her Michael Jackson shirt.

"You like Michael Jackson?" he asks, moving to the side so she can close and lock the door.

"Love him." Mickie replies. "This was one of the first gifts Ben gave me." She blushes and looks up at Paul, but he just smiles and leads the way to his truck.

After helping her in – *seriously, what a gentleman!* – and getting in himself, he starts the truck before saying, "You don't have to feel bad every time you say Ben's name. He was obviously important to you. How long had you been together?"

Mickie really appreciates his way of handling this. She always tried so hard not to mention Ben when she was on dates, but it was true – he had been important to her. "So, we got married right after I graduated high school, and he was killed in a drunk driving accident on the Fourth of July of that year; so, we were only married a few weeks."

Was it her imagination or had his grip on the wheel tightened when she spoke of the accident? "However, Ben and I basically grew up together. We went to the same elementary, middle, and high school. We were friends and became closer in middle school and started dating in eighth grade. We were together from then on." Mickie smiles a small, sad smile as she reminisces.

"Wow," Paul breathes. "That's a really long relationship. And his parents thought you cheated on him or slept with a guy within weeks of his passing?"

Mickie glances at him, remembering how protective he had been last week when she had mentioned that. "Yeah, my parents couldn't believe it, either. But Ben's parents were never the same after the accident. They were so angry. And I don't think they ever thought I was good enough for Ben. They wanted Ben to go to college and be a big shot. That wasn't Ben's dream, but it was theirs and Ben had not told them that he wasn't planning to go in the fall. We just wanted to be married, start a family, and live happily ever after. Neither of us had crazy aspirations and I think his parents blamed that on me."

Changing the subject, Mickie asks, "So, Paul...where are we headed today?"

Paul smiles and turns into the parking lot of what looks like a golf club. Mickie bends below the visor to read **Blaine's Shooting Range**.

"A shooting range?!?" Mickie squeaks.

Paul turns off the truck and turns towards her. "You said you were vanilla, and you didn't seem to like it. One of the things on that list was shooting a gun. I don't own a gun, and since you never shot one, figured you didn't either. This is an easy way to cross something off your list." He's looking at her resolutely and Mickie can't help but slowly smile a huge smile.

"Let's do it!"

Once inside, they show their IDs to the man at the desk and then follow the attendant to the prep room. They watch a short instructional video and then the attendant gets them earmuffs and safety goggles. Paul had experience with shooting a gun, so the attendant spends little time with him; but Mickie is both nervous and excited.

They first go to the inside range and the instructor asks to see Paul's stance. Once the instructor approves Paul, he starts shooting. Mickie is impressed he knows so much – his background is definitely different from hers and she needs to know more about him. Paul is decent: never hitting the bull's eye but hitting the target almost every time.

Mickie needs help. Even though she watched the video and listened to the instructions, she still doesn't hold the gun properly or have the right stance. Finally, after the instructor positions her correctly, she's free to shoot. Her first shot is way off, but she calms down, closes an eye, and aims; her last shot makes it into the yellow circle.

"I did it!" Mickie screams. She puts down her gun and turns towards Paul, "I hit the mark! I did it!" Paul had been watching and smiles at her. Mickie hops towards him and gives him a huge hug, then backs away but at once gives him another one.

"I'm sorry, but not really. I'm just so excited! Thank you so much, Paul!" She smiles up at him and momentarily forgets the instructor is still there. *I want to kiss him*, she realizes. She steps back. "Can we go again?"

Paul grins and responds, "yeah, but we still have the outside range as well."

Chapter Twelve: Patrick's Not-Quite-a-Senior Skip Day

Patrick pulls into the little driveway and parks his truck. He pulls out his cellphone, but he can just make out Karen closing the door behind her in the early morning light. She gives him a huge smile and waves her bejeweled hand. Patrick smiles back and wonders how she and Mickie can be best friends when they are such opposites.

Karen pulls open the door and gets in. "Did you tell her we're coming?"

Patrick puts the truck in reverse and heads out. "No, just like you said."

Karen gives a quiet squeal then turns back to look at him. "You know she'll refuse at first."

Patrick smiles and grins wickedly at Karen, "That's where you come in."

Karen laughs good-naturedly and leans back in her seat. "At least I know why you reached out to me. Don't get me wrong, I was stoked when I saw your friend request. But I was wondering what you would be contacting me for after all this time. Especially since you've been seeing Mickie."

Patrick grins; he likes Karen. He pulls in front of Mickie's house and parks the car. "OK, so I'm going to call her, and I'll put it on the speakerphone so you can hear. Don't make a sound though. Just wave at her when you see her." Karen nods and Patrick hits "call" under Mickie's name. It rings twice before Mickie answers it.

"Good morning? Everything OK?" Mickie sounds slightly concerned but also quiet; he realizes she must have him on the speakerphone as well since she must still be getting ready.

"Yeah, everything's fine. Great, in fact. I thought I'd surprise you with a day out." Patrick replies, trying to keep a straight face as Karen hides her face in the crook of her elbow to keep from laughing.

"Oh. Oh, how sweet. But I work weekday mornings. I'm actually just getting ready to head out."

"Yeah," Patrick responds, "I know, but I thought...I can't give you a school day to skip but I could help you skip a day of work." The sentence hangs in the air as he senses Mickie putting the pieces together.

"Oh..." *Patrick imagines her blushing as she considers what he's suggesting.* "I really can't. I didn't skip school because it wasn't the right thing to do. Skipping work is even worse...right?"

"Well, call it a mental health day then. When was the last time you called off work? They will manage without you. Come on." Patrick is trying to wheedle her into making the decision herself, without Karen's involvement; although Karen is already miming at him, asking if she should speak up yet.

"I don't know...I really don't think I can. It's sweet of you –"

"Oh, come on, Mickie! Don't make me hurt you so you have a real reason to call off! It's just for one day and to have some fun with friends." Apparently, Karen could not contain herself any longer.

"Karen?!?!?" Mickie's voice is much louder now. Patrick guesses she picked up the phone when she heard her best friend's voice.

"Yeah! Now come on. We'll give you moral support while you call your manager and say you won't make it in, if you really need us to, but we're going to paint the town red with you in tow whether you like it or not!" Patrick's not sure picking Karen up beforehand was the best idea now. This wasn't how he had wanted this to go.

"Hey, Mickie, it's Paul again. Yes, Karen is in the truck with me. She was SUPPOSED to stay silent so you could make the choice on your own, but that went down the drain. I promise I'll hold her back from hurting you." Karen rolls her eyes at him. "And we won't be painting the town red – whatever that means. I figured going out for breakfast, but not where you work, maybe walk through the park, then head to the zoo for the day. The three of us, all day. But I think you could count this in place of skipping school. It's definitely more risky than skipping on Senior Skip Day." He stops and waits, not realizing he's holding his breath or that Karen is watching him curiously.

They hear Mickie take a deep breath and then, "OK, I'll call Sean and tell him I can't come in today. What should I say for a reason?"

"Nothing, you've worked there for over twenty years and are the most reliable waitress he ha – he shouldn't even ask you for a reason," Karen responds.

"If he asks for a reason, you can go with the age-old excuse of not feeling well and it sounds like he would not question you. If you don't want to lie, say something came up and you should be back tomorrow," Paul answers, a little more helpfully.

"Should be?!? Are you kidnapping me or something?" Mickie sounds incredulous and gives a nervous laugh.

"No," Patrick chuckles. "That's just so he knows it's nothing serious and not to ask any more questions."

"Now hurry up," Karen shouts. "I want some pancakes swimming in syrup!"

~~~~~~

It takes Mickie about five more minutes, but then she comes out. She had called off work without a hitch and changed into more comfortable clothes. She climbs into the truck and Patrick drives them to a pancake house in the next town over. They goof by drowning them in syrup and seeing who can sop up the most syrup with one bite (Patrick wins). After breakfast, they visit a Metropark (there are tons around Michigan) and walk around, trying to be the first to spot wildlife. It's a weekday and still early enough that few are out besides joggers and bird watchers. Karen walks up to a bird watcher and asks if he can help them know what birds they are seeing and hearing. The guy goes on a little too long, but it's educational and seems to make Mickie feel a little better about skipping work.

Patrick then drives them to the zoo. Without any little kids or any further plans, they just wander around, see what they want when they want, stop for breaks, then continue. Did you know there are shows at the zoo? They go to all the live shows and to the 3D movie. They eat lunch at one of the restaurants and get snacks throughout the afternoon. They even sit for caricature drawings! The afternoon flies by and soon it's closing time. Karen and Mickie are laughing as they walk. Patrick smiles as he knows there is still one more trick up his sleeve.

Chapter Thirteen: Mickie's Love Song

Mickie could not believe the day she had just experienced. Basically, her best friend and – *what should she call Paul, are they dating now?* – Paul coerced her into skipping work, and it had been the best day of her life… or at least the best day in years. Calling off was terrible (*seriously, her hands had gotten clammy, and her BUTT had started to sweat!*), but they were right – Sean had not even questioned her; he had just said to take it easy and if she needed tomorrow off as well, just to let him know as soon as possible. She could hardly believe how easy it had been!

They started off at a pancake house, went to a Metropark, then the zoo. Mickie always had loved zoos, but as Jacob had gotten older, he had been less interested in them, so they had gone less. It had been ten years since Mickie had last gone to the zoo and it was so incredible. Now it was dinner time and Paul had yet to tell them where he was taking them. Honestly, even though it had been an amazing day, Mickie was getting tired and hoped it wasn't anywhere fancy that would take them a while to get seated and served.

"Alright, we're here," Paul announces as he pulls into a large parking lot. **Zucker's Tavern**. Oh no, this could not be happening! Mickie could not stomach bars. The last time she had been in one, she had fainted from a panic attack and security had revived her!

"Um, Paul, I'm sorry" Mickie stutters, "but I really don't do bars. Bad memories. I'm really sorry." Mickie feels terrible and hopes this doesn't put a damper on the day. She had assumed he was on the wagon as well since he had not had a drink during their first meeting. Maybe she was wrong. Maybe he was more like Karen. *Oh, why did she have to be so vanilla!*

"Mickie, listen to me," Paul grabs Mickie's hand and turns her to face him – not particularly comfortable in a truck with three people. "It's not like a bar to go hook up or get drunk. This is more upscale than that. I'm not going to say there might not be drunks, but there won't be many, and they won't get to you. And you don't have to get a drink. I'll stick with a Diet. But they have amazing burgers and pretzels here. Plus, it's early in the evening – people don't go getting drunk at family bars this early. Please, just try it. Pretend it's Applebee's." Paul smiles reassuringly and Mickie relaxes.

"OK, I'll try. I can do this. You're right. We're not going in for drinks, just dinner, and it's not just a bar. I can do this." Mickie realizes she said that last sentence aloud and blushes, but Paul squeezes her hand.

"OK, let's go. I'm starving after all that walking at the zoo!" Karen exclaims, already clambering out of the truck.

~~~~~~

It had been an enjoyable time. Paul's friend, Tom, had met them and the four of them had really enjoyed dinner. Paul was right, the hamburger and fries were amazing. All the food was amazing. And everyone had ordered a Cola (even Karen!), so it really did feel more like a restaurant than a bar. Mickie was just wondering when they would be leaving when the lights dimmed, and a bright light shone on a stage.

"Good evening, everyone! Thanks for coming out for karaoke night! I see some familiar faces and a few new ones. Welcome to all. The way we do things here: there is a sign-up sheet up here on the piano next to a book of songs I can perform. Print your name and the song. We'll go in the order written. Don't be nervous if this is your first time – we're all rock stars here!" There was whooping and a scraping of chairs as people went to sign up.

"What's going on?" Mickie asks.

"It's karaoke night!" Karen screams, already rushing to join the queue. Mickie turns to Paul.

"I'm going to the bathroom. Excuse me" Tom says, pushing back and going the opposite direction of Karen and the throng.

"Mickie…" Paul begins.

"Don't Mickie me. Look, it's one thing to take me to a shooting range. I can even oversee basically kidnapping me and making me skip work. But this… this is public embarrassment. You can't make me go up in front of all these people and sing." Mickie realizes her voice is rising, but she's barely holding back tears.

"OK, first off, you're not a child, so it wasn't kidnapping," Paul tries again. Mickie folds her arms and glares at him. "Secondly, no one is going to make you go up and sing." Mickie relaxes a little but still looks on guard. "However," Paul continues, again reaching out to take her hand, "I would strongly encourage you to try. We're far enough away from Hadad that no one here knows you and they will never see you or think of you ever again. It's a karaoke bar, on a school night – no one here is Michael Jackson. Yes, this is a step up from shooting a gun or skipping work, but I really think you'll regret it if you don't at least try." He has her there. Even now, Mickie is wondering what song she could sing in front of strangers… and Paul.

"What about you?" Mickie asks. "Are you going to sing?"

"I'll sign up if you do," Paul challenges. Mickie hesitates then grins.

"OK," she takes a deep breath and stands up, "let's do this. Do you have a go-to song?"

"Uh, no. I have actually never done this. But I figure a quick look through his book should help."

Mickie laughs. They get up and look through his book. Paul prints his name along with "Ice, Ice Baby." "You know that whole song? You can rap it?" Mickie asks, impressed.

Paul laughs, "I guess you'll have to wait and see." Mickie prints her name and then "Man! I Feel Like a Woman." Paul's smile lights up his face, "That'll be a great hit."

"You think so?" Mickie sounds nervous.

"Definitely. But I also think you'll do great." And he grabs her hand as they walk back to their table. Turns out, Tom wasn't sticking around for karaoke – maybe he was worried Paul would challenge him to sing as well. The singing was surprisingly good! Karen killed it with "Wannabe" and signed up for another song at the end. As Karen was up front singing, Paul reached out to hold Mickie's hand. When the pianist announced that Paul was on deck with "Ice, Ice Baby" he squeezed her hand and walked up front.

"So," Karen sings as soon as Paul is out of earshot. "We're to hand holding now. Will he be dropping me off first tonight?" she waggles her eyebrows suggestively at Mickie.

"Will you stop!" Mickie laughs, lightly smacking Karen. "He's just being supportive. Honestly, I don't even know if we're officially dating yet – he hasn't asked me."

"Oh, please!" Karen scoffs. "He's asked you out on a date and now he's going through some sort of bucket list, taking you along with him. Of course, you're dating!"

Mickie warms, partly from blushing and partly from joy. Karen didn't know that Paul was using a Never Have I Ever list, or that he was using one because Mickie had shared on their first date about being so vanilla compared to that list. Paul was being gentle yet pushy, as they plodded their way through the list. With a jolt, Mickie remembers a specific item on that list and blushes deeper, just as Paul gets up on stage. Paul is amazing. You can tell he knows this song inside and out. And he has a nice voice. Rap is not Mickie's cup of tea usually, but she could drink from his cup any day. *Oh man, was she thinking like Karen?*

As Paul climbs off the stage, he gives her hand a squeeze. "Just relax. You can barely see the audience. Just pretend you're singing at home, and no one can see or hear you."

Mickie climbs up on stage, squeezing the mic tightly in both sweaty hands. As the music begins, Mickie takes a deep breath and tries to draw on her inner Shania. "Let's go girls." It comes out weak, but she hears whistles from the audience. She tries to just fall into the music and sing a song she has been singing since she was a teenager. Once she finishes, she hears roaring and is afraid she's about to pass out from another panic attack but realizes it's clapping and cheering from the audience. She smiles and walks back to her seat. Karen hugs her before she gets to the table.

"You did it! You did it! You actually did it! And you NAILED it!" Karen is hugging and squealing, quite beside herself.

Mickie smiles at Paul who is already smiling at her. "Told you, you could do it. And the audience loved you. You want to do another?"

"No," Mickie says quickly, sitting down slightly shakily; however, she can't keep back a giddy grin when she adds, "But maybe another time."

Chapter Fourteen: Patrick Meets the Family

Patrick cleans up before calling it a day. He's feeling good until Tom comes over.

"So," Tom begins. "What bucket list item are you checking off this week?"

Patrick frowns. "Why do you want to know? I thought you still thought this was a bad idea."

"I do," Tom acknowledges, "But it's like one of my mom's soap operas – I still want to know what happens each week." He grins wickedly, baiting Patrick.

Patrick sighs. "Nothing this week. She actually texted me this morning asking if I could come over tonight and… and meet her son." Patrick refuses to meet Tom's eyes.

Tom shakes his head. "How long are you going to lead this poor broad on for? You need to tell her the truth soon, before one of you falls in love."

"I'm not falling in love," Patrick intones. "I just want to give her some happy memories before…"

"Before you break her heart again?" Tom at least has the decency to look and sound sympathetic.

"Yeah," Patrick mutters, shutting his locker door harder than usual. The sound reverberates as they sit there, hearing the truth in the silence.

"Look, man, just tell her. Get it over with – like ripping off a Band-Aide. Do it tonight. The two of us can just go to the event and have seats on either side for our food and drinks." Tom claps Patrick on the shoulder. "I'll be free tonight, if you need anything."

Patrick pulls in Mickie's driveway, behind a black Kia Soul. *Great*, Patrick thinks, *A level-headed man. I can't tell her tonight with her son here! Or maybe he will beat me up and she will feel better. Plus, he would be here to comfort her. OK, Tom's right. Like ripping off a Band-Aide... one attached to the hairiest area of the arm.* He rings the doorbell. Mickie opens the door, and he can't help but notice the difference these past weeks have made. She's wearing a small amount of makeup, her hair has highlights and is hanging down her back, and she's wearing jeans and a billowy blouse. *She looks happier*, he realizes.

"Hey!" Mickie smiles. "Come in, come in. They're in the living room." *They*? Patrick walks in and then follows Mickie around the corner to the living room. A young man and lady are sitting on the couch next to each other. As soon as Patrick and Mickie walk in the room, the young couple stop talking and look up. The girl gets to her feet with a smile and comes to shake hands with Patrick.

"Paul! Nice to meet you. I'm Mara." The young lady is very pretty and clearly tries to make everyone feel comfortable. Patrick looks at the young man who comes to stand next to this young lady. He knows they are both sizing the other one up. Patrick barely remembers the picture of Ben, but this young man looks like the hazy image he remembers. He also feels the young man's distrust.

"Hey," the young man holds out his hand and grips Patrick's hand with a tighter than necessary squeeze. "My name's Jacob. Mickie's my mom."

"Nice to meet you; both of you" Patrick corrects. His walls are up and suddenly he feels caged. "Your mom has told me so much about you – you two must be really close."

"Well, I've had to be the man of the house for a long time. I just want to make sure she's safe and happy." Jacob is still watching Patrick intently, and Patrick wonders if this boy guesses something is up. *How could he though? He wasn't even born yet!*

"Oh, Jacob," Mickie laughs nervously.

"What?" Jacob turns to his mother. "You've been acting different these past few weeks and I find out it's because of the guy you're dating. I'm going to come meet him." Mickie blushes but doesn't look away from her son.

"Maybe I'm starting to live a little," Mickie challenges.

"Maybe," Jacob interrupts. "But it's a pretty big change in a short amount of time. Besides, shouldn't I want to meet the man who may become my stepfather?"

"JACOB!" Both women yell at him, glaring. Mickie shifts her gaze to Patrick who realizes he's yet to move or react to anything.

"Jacob, why don't we go walk the block?" Mara asks, guiding him towards the door. Jacob turns his glare from his mother to Patrick then shrugs and walks outside with his girlfriend. The door slams shut, and Mickie turns to Patrick with tears in her eyes.

"Paul, I'm so sorry," she begins, but Patrick cuts her off. He pulls her into a hug.

"Mickie, I get it. He's scared, uncertain, and protective. Let's get you a cup of water and then I'll go out and talk with him."

"No!" Mickie pushes against Patrick's chest and looks up at him. "I had no idea he was going to act like this. I think it's best if you just leave. I'm really sorry." Patrick looks at Mickie and remembers what Tom is expecting him to do. He sighs and lifts his hand to push a strand of hair behind Mickie's ear. She leans into his cupped hand and looks up. They are close together.

He feels her step forward and lean up on her tiptoes. He feels his hand go behind her neck as he leans down. He feels her breath right before touching her lips.

"Mom, I'm - WHAT THE HECK?!?" Jacob is standing in the doorway of the kitchen glaring at them as Mickie jumps backwards.

"Jacob! I –" Mickie falters, at a loss for words. Jacob turns and storms back out the front door, Patrick following him.

"Jacob! Jacob, hold up, please." Patrick hates sounding like he's begging when he feels the dominance struggle, but something else is clearly controlling him right now. Jacob turns around, glaring at Patrick.

"What do you want? Go back to making out with my mom."

"Jacob, look, I'm sorry you had to see that. Can you please just let me talk to you, man to man, for a moment?" Patrick waits for a beat, but since Jacob is still standing there, he figures that's permission enough. "OK, thanks. First off, your mom and I are nowhere near a discussion on marriage."

"Could have fooled me," Jacob mutters.

"It's rude to interrupt," Patrick intones and waits until Jacob looks at him. "No one wants to walk in on a parent kissing. If it makes you feel better, that was our first kiss."

Jacob looks up again and mutters, "sorry." Patrick nods his acknowledgment. "Why don't you tell me what's really bothering you? Maybe I can ease your discomfort."

"Why are you doing these crazy type dates instead of the typical dinner dates? Why my mom?"

"Why your mom? Honestly, kid, I just feel this tug towards her. The more I get to know her, the happier I want to make her." Patrick pauses but Jacob is still looking at him. Patrick sighs. "Your mom shared about this Never Have I Ever thing on our first date, which was a dinner date, by the way. Anyways, she seemed really upset about it, so I looked it up and started figuring out ways to help her check some off." Jacob is still looking unconvinced.

"Why?"

"I told you; I want to make her happy."

"But why? Do you two know each other from before?"

Patrick hesitates. "No. No, of course not." Jacob narrows his eyes, and Patrick can tell he doesn't believe him. "Look, next Saturday I'm taking your mom to an event – hopefully she will meet someone famous and should end up on TV because of the seats I got. Why don't you and your girlfriend join us? I got four tickets." Patrick can't believe he just invited this mistrusting boy, but he had to do something. That look… it scared Patrick.

Jacob continues to watch Patrick before nodding and loosening his stance. "OK, sure." Then he smiles and Patrick can finally see Mickie in the boy. "Let's go back inside so the women stop worrying I'm gonna hit you. Does my mom know about the event yet? What is it? Can I tell her? She'll be pretty upset with me."

Patrick smiles and claps Jacob on the shoulder. "Sure, kid. See if that softens her up. And no, I don't tell dates until we're there – part of the excitement."

Chapter Fifteen: Mickie Gets Some TLC

Friday, early morning

Mickie's phone vibrates as she dresses for the morning.

Paul: Can't wait for tonight.

Paul: Dress comfortably (shorts and T-shirt fine).

Paul: Wish I could pick you up and drive you myself.

Grinning, Mickie picks up the phone and responds, *I know. Me too. But it was nice of you to invite Jacob and Mara and it makes more sense for the three of us to meet you there. You still won't tell me what it is yet?*

Paul: Nope. And I'll send the address to Jacob after lunch so hopefully you will be surprised. ;)

With a bounce in her step, Mickie continues getting ready.

Friday early afternoon

Mickie's phone starts playing "Wind Beneath My Wings" as she pulls it from her purse. "Hey, Jacob! You got the address?"

"Yeah, mom, I did. It's at Little Caesar's Arena –"

"Ooh, how exciting! I wonder whose concert?!?"

"It's not a concert mom, it's –"

"Oh! Don't tell me! I want to be surprised." Mickie smiles broadly, bouncing on the balls of her feet.

"Mom, are you sure? Because I'm pretty sure you'll never guess."

"Oh! Even better! Doesn't he come up with the BEST surprises?!?"

"Uh… sure mom, we'll go with that."

Mickie is oblivious to the sarcasm in Jacob's voice as she tells him that Paul told her to dress comfortably.

"OK, mom… Mara and I will pick you up at five, then –"

"4:30, OK? I don't want to be late because of traffic and keep Paul waiting."

There's a moment's hesitation before Jacob responds, "OK, mom. We'll pick you up at 4:30. See you then."

"See you soon, honey! Love you!"

"Love you too, mom."

Friday, about 5:45pm

"I can't believe how much traffic there's been! I'm so glad we left earlier or else we would be late. Oh, hurry, Jacob! We're almost there. I can't wait to see the marquis and know what we're in for!" Mickie wrings her hands slightly, as she fiddles with her purse handles. Paul has already texted, and she's later than she likes to be. They still need to park, find Paul, get refreshments, and get to their seats and she doubts they can do it in less than fifteen minutes. As they round the bend, she sees Little Caesar's Arena and the flashing marquis shows a shirtless man she has never seen before. Below the buff man's picture flashes WELCOME WWE! "WWE?" Mickie sounds aloud, mystified.

"Yeah, mom, WWE." Jacob lets it hang in the air like she should know what that is, but she doesn't; luckily, Mara clarifies, "Professional wrestling." Mickie's jaw drops, but no words spill out. At that moment, they see Paul waving at them. "I'll drop you off here, mom. Mara and I can miss the beginning. Just text us where the seats are." Mickie climbs out and walks over to Paul as Jacob drives to the parking garage.

"Finally! I'm glad I got here early. I should have told Jacob to leave earlier. These things are always so packed." Paul leads Mickie inside where security checks her purse, then they get in line for refreshments. "I'm not sure we'll have time to get food and drinks; we might miss something. Are you surprised?" Paul cranes his head to look at the line of people and taps his toes before looking over at Mickie.

"Yes," is all Mickie can get out. She shakes her head and looks around her. "All these people are here for wrestling? There isn't another event?" She's hoping he will laugh and tell her about a concert or magician who is also here and of course he would not bring her, Jacob, and Mara to a wrestling event, but unfortunately...

"Yeah, people go crazy for WWE. And it doesn't come to Detroit all that often, so we're lucky. This line is barely moving, and it's 6:25, are you sure you don't want to just go to our seats?" Paul looks at Mickie hopefully, but she's still in shock with the turn of events.

"I... No, I think we should get refreshments now; plus, maybe Jacob and Mara will find us easier out here – " A roar erupts from the nearest entrance, causing Mickie to jump, as the speakers announce a guy's name. The noise continues to stay around a roar level. Mickie restrains herself from covering her ears, but only barely. She realizes she's gritting her teeth and scrunching her shoulders up, so she appears to have no neck. She tries to force her body to appear relaxed.

Paul leans over and pulls her to him, speaking into her ear so she can hear, "I thought this was Smackdown, but it's Smackdown Live. So, I don't think we can get on TV. But I got us floor seats, so maybe we'll be able to speak to one of the superstars or touch their hands!" Paul leans back, smiling, but then tilts his head as he registers Mickie's lack of enthusiasm. "Is everything OK?" Paul asks, creases beginning to appear on his forehead.

Mickie feels awful. "Yeah!" She half yells back, then beckons for him to lean closer so she can speak normally into his ear, "I've never been to a wrestling event or even watched WWE, so I'm just in shock of all this." Paul jerks back, a range of emotions readable on his face: shock, fear, confusion, wariness. "It's OK!" Mickie says loudly, squeezing his hand. "I hadn't shot a gun until you took me to the range, and I had a blast" Paul smiles and nods his head, squeezing Mickie's hand back. They get their drinks and snacks as Jacob and Mara enter. Paul leads them to their seats.

The night goes by well. Paul tries to fill them in on who the superstars are. Mickie eventually stops cringing every time a new superstar comes out and fireworks go off. She can't believe the outfits, or lack of outfits, these people wear, but the moves are impressive. The women really intrigue her. Mickie would never wear what they wear, but they exude a confidence she envies. And the women are as athletic and ruthless as the men! By the end of the night, Mickie is smiling and clapping as the lights come on. She didn't try to touch any of the superstars, although most of the fans around her did, and one lady was almost crying because she had touched one's hand.

"Well?" Paul asks, smiling despite his obvious nerves.

Mickie smiles broader and replies, "That was like nothing I've ever seen before!"

"It kind of takes your breath away," Mara remarks.

"Yeah, nothing like seeing mostly naked strangers duke it out in a ring" Jacob sarcastically responds.

The girls shoot Jacob a look, but Paul returns his sarcastic comment with some pent-up frustration of his own. "It's not like I invited you all to TLC." They all stare at him and he goes slightly red before interpreting, "Tables, Ladders, and Chairs. It's a pay-per-view event they used to have."

"Yeah, good thing you didn't" Jacob agrees. "We would think you're taking us for some tender, loving care and would have been even more shocked." Mara snorts but tries to hide it behind a fake cough.

"Look, it's good to try new things. The polite thing to say, Jacob, is thank you." Mickie intones with warning.

Jacob looks around then shrugs his shoulders, "Thanks for the new experience, <u>Paul</u>." Although no one misses the sarcasm, no one brings it up, either. Paul shakes his head before grabbing Mickie's hand and leading them out.

Once they enter the parking garage, Paul and Mickie fall back, so Jacob can lead them to his car. "I'm sorry. I grew up on WWE. I didn't think it'd be something scandalous." Paul rubs his thumb over Mickie's hand. She squeezes his hand. "Don't mind Jacob. I think he was just shocked and possibly uncomfortable with bringing Mara here." Mickie lets go of Paul's hand as another car drives past them, then puts her arm around his waist and leans in for a sideways hug. "It was definitely shocking," she chuckles, "but by the end, I was kind of enjoying it." Paul kisses the top of her head as Jacob and Mara stop at the car. Mickie moves her arm, but Paul grabs her face and kisses her, hard and quick. "Hope you enjoyed your TLC," Paul says over his shoulder to Jacob. He kisses the top of Mickie's forehead goodbye then walks off to his car, the three of them just staring after him.

Chapter Sixteen: Mickie, Don't Be a Karen

"What the heck!" Jacob fumes, as the paralysis spell breaks over their trio and Paul disappears.

Turning towards her son, Mickie's eyebrows pinch together. "Don't yell and don't say heck – there's no need to talk like that." Turning, Mickie opens the door to get in the car. Mara looks from Jacob to Mickie then back to Jacob, before saying, "Mickie, why don't you sit up front this time? I have a feeling you and Jacob will be talking." They all get in the car, tension palpable.

As they start to drive, Jacob says, in a calm, yet sarcastic voice, "I don't think my saying 'heck' is the worst word we have heard tonight. If this is what Paul likes for entertainment, I hope you now agree with my reservations."

Mickie stiffens in the front seat, sitting straight as possible and looking ahead. "It was definitely different, but this doesn't change the way I feel. Honestly, it makes sense. He grew up harsher than we did. He's from a rougher background and part of Michigan. This is what he grew up on, and so he didn't think anything of inviting us to it. Once he realized I had no idea about wrestling, he looked nervous. He's trying to give me a life worth talking about. I don't see what you have against him."

"What do I have against him?!? First off, I know he's hiding something. You know too little about him. He tries too hard. He's definitely hiding something, and you should be smart enough to see this and demand to know what it is." Knuckles white around the steering wheel, Jacob takes a breath.

"He's a nice man! I brought up on our first date about fearing I'm too vanilla, and he has taken it upon himself to fix that for me. Why is that so hard for you to wrap your mind around? Why must you assume he's hiding something and making up for a past wrong?"

"Because, mom, it's strange. Why would a middle-aged man care what a stranger thought of herself? Why not just assume she would be easy bait and seduce her?"

"So, you'd rather us be sleeping around rather than going on strange dates?"

"Ew, no. Don't be Karen."

Mickie's mouth drops indignantly. "Excuse me?!?"

"Mom, I know she's your best friend and she's nice, but she's loose. She has had, what, three divorces? And I'm pretty sure she's slept with more than just those three guys."

"What does her sex life have to do with our conversation?" Mickie hisses.

Jacob senses he has crossed a line, but also possibly struck a chord. "Mom, you're a good woman. You had one sweetheart whom you married right after high school. You worked hard to support us as a single mom with hardly any support. You rarely dated and no guy ever seemed a good fit. Why is that?"

Jacob pauses to glance at Mickie before continuing, "Is it really because they didn't continue things with you? You could have reached out to them if you had wanted. You never miss work. Never rock the boat. You're steady. Dependable. Hardworking. You seem independent. Have you really wanted a committed relationship?"

Mickie began to relax during Jacob's speech. She has been looking at him and finally starts to see things from his point of view.

Slowly, she begins to answer him, "I think I see what you've been seeing... or at least, I think I'm starting to see things from your point of view. I never went looking for another man, but I have been lonely. I love you and love the life we've built, but it's time for you to start living a separate life and that has really thrown my loneliness into sharp perspective." Mickie stops again, reflecting on the conversation with Karen last month, the night she had met Paul. Maybe she _had_ been depressed.

"I don't want to live alone," Mickie whispers, lips quivering. "I don't want to be an old spinster. But I don't want to burden you, either. I want you to live your life, independent of me. Still visit and stay connected, but live. Start your own home and family. And I'm happy that seems to be working for you."

With this last statement, Mickie looks back at Mara, both women teary-eyed. "I want to live my own life, too," Mickie continues. "But I want to share it with someone. A sweetheart, as you so tenderly put it." Mickie pauses, thinking about Ben: of all the time they had together, all the dreams they had, and how it ended so quickly.

"Yes, Paul is different than us. He looks different, talks a little differently, acts a little differently, and apparently enjoys different things than us." Mickie smirks as Jacob rolls his eyes. "But he cares about me. He saw past a lonely, middle-aged woman with a grown son and heard what I was expressing. I wanted a life worth living. I love you, Jacob," Mickie reaches out, placing her hand on Jacob's arm. "But I gave up everything to give you the best life I could give. I don't regret it for an instant, but I'm ready to explore and live my life. Paul gives me that, while respectfully keeping his distance in the sex department. All we've done is kiss, and, unfortunately, you've seen both." Mickie half laughs, squeezing Jacob's arm. "Now, if you quit giving him a hard time, I think he'd lay off the PDA," Mickie quips, removing her hand and fully facing Jacob.

Jacob drives quietly for a few moments, contemplating everything he has heard. He supposes he has given Paul a harder time than necessary. And he has been acting like a spoiled child around his mom. He slowly gives Mickie a half smile before turning his attention back to the road. "OK, mom. I'll try to warm up to the guy. But I don't think I'll be getting into WWE with him."

Mickie laughs and the tension finally dissipates from the vehicle.

Chapter Seventeen: Patrick Gets Permanent

Patrick paces his apartment, tongue between his teeth, before grabbing his car keys and walking out the door. He's nervous- more nervous than he has been about the other dates. This was a big one, a permanent one. "Relax," he mumbles to himself, starting the truck. "What's the worst that can happen? She says absolutely not, and you guys go have a normal date."

This has been in the works for a while. When he decided to help Mickie cross off items from that list, there were several that he knew would take weeks to reserve and this was one of them. Luckily, the WWE event had been coming to Detroit this summer, so he had just needed to buy tickets.

"Yeah, let's not reflect on that while I'm nervous," he mutters to himself. He releases his death grip on the steering wheel, reflecting on their last date. It was bad enough that Mickie had no idea what WWE was (*how embarrassing*), but then Jacob had just been horrible about it. Patrick knew he should not have left as he did – but Jacob needed to learn his place. Patrick wasn't going to leave Mickie alone, just because her grown son didn't like him.

Patrick pulls into Mickie's little driveway and inhales deeply before blowing it out. Opening his door, he sees Mickie already locking up, so he goes to open the passenger side. "Hey."

Mickie smiles and stands on tiptoe, lightly kissing him. He stares at her as she smiles back and gets in the truck. "Evening."

Patrick walks over to his side and turns to look at her once he buckles. "What just happened?"

"What do you mean?" Mickie giggles, a soft blush creeping up her neck.

"You kissed me."

"Yeah."

"Oh. OK, then." Patrick is completely at a loss for words.

"I thought, with the way you left at the arena, that that would be OK," Mickie starts, trailing off and looking uncertainly at Patrick.

"It is! I just... you caught me off guard," he also leaves his sentence hanging. "So, um... you ready to go?"

"Yeah!"

They drive in silence. Patrick knows he should say something, but what? *This is getting too serious!* Maybe he should just take her out to eat tonight? *Calm down!*

"A t-tat-too parlor?" Mickie stammers, looking out the windshield at the shop they had just pulled in front of.

"Yeah... unless, if you don't want to..." *Breathe!* "It was on the list. You seemed to like mine. I reserved this time for you to get one, but if you don't want to, we can leave."

Mickie stares at the shop, then turns to Patrick. "Let's go in."

Inside is darker than outside. There's a couple of tattoo artists joking in the back. There is another artist working on a man in the corner. Another lady greets them at the counter. "Reservation?"

"Yeah, Mickie Brenner."

Mickie grabs Patrick's hand and squeezes; he squeezes back.

"Which one of you is Mickie?"

"I am," Mickie squeaks out.

"Do you know what you want?"

"N-no. D-do you have a book?"

"Yeah, sure." The lady pulls a book from under the counter and sets it on top. "Most people look online though. Pick a picture or give me an idea and I can draw something up." She walks away and Patrick and Mickie go to sit in chairs by the door.

Mickie is slowly turning pages when she asks Patrick, "How did you know what to get – when you got your tattoo?"

Patrick goes rigid, remembering the sound of crunching metal, the despair of alienation, the hope of forgiveness through Christ. "I went through a rough patch. I came out a better person. I wanted something to remind me of that."

Mickie puts down the book and pulls out her phone. "I know I want a flower. But something that stands for new beginnings, or resilience..." again she trails off. "What about a tulip? What do you think of this?" She shows an image on her phone to Patrick who nods, smiling.

"What does it stand for?"

"Rebirth." Mickie watches him, then continues, "I feel like that's what's happening to me. I never realized how depressed I was, even though looking back, it was obvious. I was just in such a funk. Then you came along. You have opened me up to a world of possibilities; pushed me out of my comfort zone. I know I'm different than before we met," she pauses.

"Yeah?"

"Maybe, it's the start of a new chapter. Heck, maybe the second half of the book."

Patrick doesn't know what to say to that. He knows what she's hinting at. But how can he commit to a sincere relationship, when he's keeping such a big secret from her? "Let's get you that tulip."

Mickie reclines on the chair. Julie, her tattoo artist, lays it flat then raises it. She lays a marker drawing above Mickie's right hip, then peels it off, leaving a purple outline of a tulip.

"Is this where you want it? Once I start, it's hard to readjust."

Mickie looks down then takes a mirror to see it reflected up. "Yeah, that's right. It won't be purple, though, will it?"

"I'll outline it in black. If you want it filled in with color, let me know."

"No, I'll, um, I'll stick with just the outline for now."

The needle whirs to life and Mickie grabs Patrick's hand. He can't believe she's being so vulnerable with him. This is a decent amount of skin, and skin that's usually covered. She squeezes his hand, hard, and he looks away from her stomach and to her face.

"You're doing great. Just remember to keep breathing."

"Yeah, if you feel faint or sick, let me know right away," Julie says, not looking up.

"I'm fine," Mickie says through gritted teeth.

It only takes about 15 minutes and Julie puts the needle away. "All done, unless you want me to fill in with color."

Mickie looks down in awe. Then, holding her shirt up in one hand and using Patrick to stand her upright with the other, she looks in the tall mirror. "Wow," she whispers.

"I always wanted a tattoo," Mickie states on the ride home. "I was afraid to get one because my parents were very against it. Then I got married right after graduation and Ben died 26 days later. Then I was a teenage, pregnant widow. Then, a young, single mom, working two jobs to make ends meet. Then… I don't know. I just forgot about me. I have been on autopilot for so many years that I stopped thinking about what I wanted. I didn't have any dreams or goals; I just lived day to day."

She pauses, caught up in all the emotions. She finally was coming to terms with her depression. But was she still depressed? She thought about the summer so far. Her hand went to her tattoo, tracing it through the cling, and she smiles. "Thank you, Paul."

Chapter Eighteen: Mickie Takes a Dip

Mickie rolls over in bed and looks at her alarm clock - 11:35PM. *Why can't I fall asleep?!?* She throws her blankets off and slides into her slippers before walking to the kitchen. "Maybe a nice cup of hot tea will help me sleep."

As she gets everything ready, she wonders what is keeping her up. "I just feel restless. Like I need to do something." Mickie usually doesn't have a problem falling asleep. She has had the same bedtime routine for years, falling asleep and waking up like clockwork. Tonight, though, it's like her blood is humming inside her. She's wide awake at a time she's usually in REM sleep. She grabs her tea and goes to sit in front of the TV but doesn't turn it on.

"I don't want to watch anything." Then she realizes she's talking to herself aloud and scowls. *Stop it, Michelle. You're a grown woman. You don't talk to yourself.* She sips her tea and closes her eyes. Maybe she will try to meditate. She can almost hear her body humming now. *Cut it out! What is wrong with you?* That's what she needs to figure out.

She closes her eyes and takes another sip. *OK, what is going on?* She takes deep breaths and relaxes. Paul comes to mind. Mickie smiles and takes another sip. Paul leans in for a kiss. The kiss turns passionate, his hands starting to move.

Mickie opens her eyes. What was she thinking? Paul was very noncommittal after her attempts to push for commitment.

Mickie bites the inside of her cheek. She kissed him when he picked her up, but he didn't really kiss her back and seemed confused when he asked her about it. When she talked about the meaning behind the tulip tattoo being rebirth, he didn't comment on it. The tattoo was on her rib cage, yet he had kept his gaze on her face during the procedure. Maybe he didn't want a committed relationship.

Am I still too vanilla? She sets the mug down on her little end table and leans forward. Paul's been great at checking off items on that list, but what if he just wants to help her and not be in a relationship with her? She traces the tulip tattoo on her hip, looks down at it, then stands up. *I'm not vanilla anymore and maybe it's time I chose the date.*

~~~~~~

Mickie: You still awake?

Paul: Yeah, everything OK?

Mickie: Yes… actually, I was wondering if I could come pick you up?

Two minutes pass.

Paul: Uh, sure. Are you sure everything is OK? I would rather know now.

Mickie: Yes, everything is fine. What's your address?

Paul: 26 Montgomery Road, Hadad

Mickie: OK, I'm leaving now.

Paul: OK

~~~~~~

Mickie gets in her car and puts his address into her phone, so it comes up on her car. *I can't believe what I'm about to do. But it's time to take charge.*

In no time at all, she pulls into an apartment complex and sees Paul waiting outside. She stops alongside him, and he gets in.

"What's going on?" he asks before the door fully closes behind him.

"You'll see," she says, typing in another address. "You know, everyone thought Ben and I were the perfect high school sweethearts, but we kept a secret from everyone." Paul looks over at Mickie but doesn't say a word. "Ben and I… we had sex. Before we got married. We were careful, but we got into the moment one night and then after the first time… well, there didn't seem to be a reason not to. Ben was religious, like you. That's the main reason we got married right after high school; he felt guilty about sleeping with me before we were married."

Mickie pauses and turns off the main road. There is at least a minute of silence before she continues. "I'm sure we would have gotten married regardless, but that was the reason why we rushed it." She pulls onto a road with houses lining a lake. She pulls into a driveway and shuts the car off, turning in her seat to look at Paul head on. "So, maybe I wasn't so vanilla after all."

"Why are you telling me this? And why are we here?" Paul asks, slowly.

"I thought I would initiate a date for once. This is my friend, Tilda's, house. She and her family live here with lakeshore access. But they're on vacation right now." She's looking at him pointedly.

"I still don't –"

"I'm going skinny dipping. This is a sleepy neighborhood, so you don't have to worry about getting the police called on you or anything. Tilda and Tristan have a dock out back, and since they're not home and the docks are relatively secluded, no one will see us."

"Us?"

"Yes. If you'll join me." With that, Mickie turns, opens her door, and walks out, gently closing the door behind her. Thankfully, Mickie hears the soft opening and closing of Paul's door just a second later.

"Are you crazy?" he whispers. "If someone sees you, they really could call the police and your son would have to bail you out. Is that really a conversation you want to have with him? And you know he'll blame me."

"If we get caught, I'll call Karen – she'll bail me out and think it's wonderful." Mickie turns and Paul almost knocks her over. He grabs her to steady them, and she grabs hold of his arms, his wonderfully strong, muscular arms.

They look at each other, Paul questioning and Mickie resolute. She has no idea where this recklessness is coming from, but it's like something inside her just snapped and this new persona has taken over.

"I'm doing this. You're welcome to join me or head back to the car." With that, she lets go of him, walks the rest of the way to the dock and pulls her shirt over her head. Without thinking, she removes the rest of her clothes, sits on the edge of the dock, closes her eyes, sucks in her lips, and slides into the water.

Even though it's August, the water is cool and not very deep – only coming up to her hips. She sinks down until it covers her shoulders and turns around.

Paul is staring at her. It's hard to see in the dark, but she feels like there's energy passing between their looks. Then, keeping his eyes on her, he takes his shirt off followed by everything else. He walks to the dock and slides in after her, also sinking down.

"Want to take a walk?" Mickie asks, trying not to dwell on what she just saw. He just looks at her and nods. She grabs his hand and takes the lead. They carefully make their way out deeper, until they can more comfortably stand, concealed, in the water. Mickie at least is fully concealed; Paul, being taller, looks like a David two-thirds submerged.

A cloud passes and moonlight bathes the lake – submerged or not, the water is clear. Mickie had been looking at Paul in the mostly dark, but now it seemed too personal. She lets go of his hand and covers her breasts, looking away from him.

"I'm sorry," she whispers. "I don't know what came over me." She waits in silence and the moonlight, unable to say or even think anything else.

"I once slept with a girl in the woods."

She turns and looks at his face, forcing herself not to look down. He steps towards her and the energy she thought she had felt earlier is palpable now. They look at each other and then a kaleidoscope of thoughts and emotions breaks over them as their bodies connect.

Chapter Nineteen: Patrick and Pastor Ted Talk

Patrick pulls into the Hadad Church of Christ's parking lot, jumps out of his truck, and books it to the door. Pastor Ted is waiting for him, holding the door open.

"Good morning, Patrick. What an unexpected blessing to see you today. I was surprised to receive your text asking if we could meet in my office, instead of our usual coffee shop." They go into his office, Pastor Ted going behind his desk to a desk chair and Patrick grabbing the lounge chair facing the desk.

"I have a confession to make," Patrick blurts out, already beginning to sweat.

Pastor Ted raises his eyebrows. "That's not how it works. You don't have to come to me to confess something. I can't forgive whatever you have done – only God can forgive sins. However, if you need someone to confide in and help with advice, I would be happy to help you."

Patrick looks at his clasped hands before lifting tortured eyes to his mentor. "I slept with her."

Pastor Ted's eyebrows raise higher. "Who is her?"

"Michelle A. Brenner."

"Brenner? Brenner... ? Isn't that the last name of the guy who died in the car accident?"

"YES!" Patrick wails, dropping his face to his hands.

Pastor Ted gives him a minute before asking, "Why don't you start with meeting her and catch me up on what's been going on."

Patrick takes a deep breath, then begins his tale, starting with meeting Mickie at Applebee's. He describes the moment he found out Mickie was Michelle and lying about who he really was: "I freaked! I told her I was in lawn service and had no idea it was her house; then, as

I was inspecting her lawn," here Patrick uses air quotes, "I called my friend Tom and had him come function as my boss and bail me out. Except then I decided to go buy her flowers and ask her out." At this, Pastor Ted leans back in his chair with a thoughtful expression, but Patrick doesn't notice and continues with his story, standing up to pace.

"I don't know. I felt this connection between us. Maybe it was her dead husband wanting us to get together. I don't know. But on that first date, she told me how she hated being so vanilla and pulled up a Never Have I Ever card – do you know what those are?"

"I do. I have two daughters who love them."

"Well, that night, after I got back to my apartment, I had the brilliant idea to take her on dates that would check those items off. I have no idea why I'm trying to give her the life she wants, but the dates have gone pretty well."

"What sort of dates?"

"Karaoke bar. Skipping work. Gun range. Tattoo. A WWE event."

Pastor Ted smirks at that one. Patrick catches it and sighs, "yeah, that one didn't go off as well." Pastor Ted smiles invitingly, and Patrick continues his tale.

"It was after the tattoo. She texted me last night asking if I was still up and said she was going to come pick me up. I had no idea what was going on. I was worried she had somehow figured out who I was. But when she picked me up, she told me about how her and Ben had had sex before getting married. That was the main reason they got married when they did and maybe she wasn't so vanilla after all. Then she parked at this swanky lakeshore house and said she was going to go skinny dipping!"

Patrick turns and faces Pastor Ted. "I honestly had no idea that's what she was planning. I have no idea what came over her. But I followed her out, trying to talk sense into her, but she just undressed! I watched her slide, naked, into the lake. Then she just looked at me, and, I don't know, it was like it was just her and me. I stripped off my clothes and followed her in. We walked until we were both mostly submerged and then the moon came out. She was back to her old self-conscience self, and I just thought, 'this is the most beautiful woman I have ever seen.'" Patrick pauses, caught up in the memory of last night.

"I closed the gap between us and we just… did it. I mean, we made out as I carried her to the shore, then we did it, but you get the picture." Patrick stammers a little, knowing he's admitting something he should not have done.

"Well," Pastor Ted begins, then stops. He looks at Patrick before leaning forward on his desk. "I think the first thing to determine is when you're going to tell this woman the truth."

"What?!?" Patrick yelps. "I just had sex with her! I can't go tell her now that I killed her husband!"

"Yes," Pastor Ted says unblinkingly, "you can. And you must."

Patrick starts pacing again, before stopping and facing Pastor Ted, "Why? How?" he asks pleadingly.

Pastor Ted gives a soft smile and motions for Patrick to have a seat. He leans towards him and softly says, "You love this woman."

Patrick just stares at him as this simple phrase washes over him. How could he love Michelle A. Brenner? He had wrecked her life. But Mickie? Patrick often caught himself replaying the dates and thinking about the next time he would see her. And last night was like no other time he had been with a woman. Yes, there was something there, but *love*?

Patrick looks into Pastor Ted's eyes, seeing compassion. "How can I tell her I love her and tell her the truth? If I tell her the truth, she'll leave me."

"You'll have to wait and see. Maybe she will be forgiving. She seems to be in love with you, as well. But you have led her on. That's your greater wrong. Once you had discovered who she was and gone back, you should have told her the truth then. Now you both are in deep, and the pain of this truth will hurt worse. For both of you. But you can't build a relationship on lies. And by withholding this truth from her, that's what you have done."

Patrick nods his head ashamedly and gets up, crossing to the door. Before leaving, he turns around and says, "I'll figure out a way. I'll find a way to tell her the truth and keep her. I'm not giving up this time," he says, fire in his eyes.

Chapter Twenty: The Sky's the Limit for Mickie

Paul and Mickie were on another one of their Never Have I Ever dates. They were getting to be more fun and comfortable each time. Or, maybe Mickie just felt that way because she was more fun and comfortable around Paul now. She smiled then told herself to pay attention to the instructor.

Today, Paul and Mickie were spending three hours at Hadad City Skydiving. There were two options for beginners: accelerated free fall or tandem free fall. Mickie had chosen accelerated free fall, where they could open their own parachute and land by themselves. The downside was they had to take a course for two hours. She didn't really mind, however, because she got to spend more time with Paul.

Just thinking his name makes her smile. She still can't quite get over what she did. She does feel a little floozy, but she would not take it back. It had been... magical. She had been like she had never been before. The confidence had been empowering. She finally felt like she and Paul were on the same level, instead of her following behind him everywhere like a sad little puppy. And the sex?!? It had been a long time, so maybe that had something to do with it, but she didn't remember it being quite so passionate. Or tender.

With Ben, sex had been quick. It had been in secret, stolen moments. Or in hiding. Or, for those brief few weeks they were married, learning about the other person's body. This had been... it had been about desire. And caring. Mickie knew Paul loved her, even though they had not said those words yet, just from the way he had treated her that night.

Mickie was finally happy. Constantly. She really had been depressed before Paul; Karen had been right. Mickie never realized how different her life could be if she decided it was something worth living. Now Mickie was living on cloud nine. *And soon,* she thinks to herself,

I'll literally be on cloud nine. Smiling at her own pun, she forces herself to pay closer attention to the instructor.

~~~~~~

"So, how are you feeling?" Paul asks Mickie as they get ready to board the plane from which they will be jumping.

"I'm pumped," she replies, bouncing on the balls of her feet. She looks up at him, grinning.

"You've been smiling a lot this morning," he notes, as they pull on their suits.

She can't tell if he's being aloof or teasing. She hopes he's happy over what happened, but what if it bothers him?

"I've just been thinking about you a lot," she says, as she bends down to tie laces, her hair shielding her face. When she straightens, he's looking right at her, a strange look on his face. Regret? He tries to hide it behind a quick smile, but the smile doesn't reach his eyes.

Her own smile falters. Thinking she might as well get it out in the open, she asks, "Are you upset over what happened?"

He smiles softly; yes, something is bothering him. He reaches out and hugs her. She lifts her head, and he's right there with a kiss, firm yet tender. "It was definitely unexpected," he says, releasing her as their instructor clears his throat. The instructor checks them, then leads them out onto the field to their plane. Paul reaches out and grabs her hand. She smiles and gently squeezes, slightly reassured.

The instructor helps them into the plane and the pilot begins their ascent. Paul leans over to Mickie, raising his voice to be heard over the noise but only just, so it's like he's only speaking into her ear. "It was wonderful. It just raised our relationship to the next level, and I don't think I was ready for that." He pauses, then adds, "But now I am."

Mickie's smile starts out slow as he begins and is so wide by the end, even those on the ground could not miss it. She knew he felt the same way!

"OK!" Their instructor yells. "We're 10,000 feet in the air now. Head over to the hanger." They stand, and Mickie doesn't know if it's the adrenaline from the height or from what Paul just told her, but she wobbles her way to the opening.

"Mickie will be jumping first; Paul, you at my command, just two seconds later. You both remember how to open your chute and land?" They nod their heads. "OK, this is the moment for any last words."

Mickie makes up her mind. As she turns to face Paul, she glimpses that look again. She shakes it off as nerves and says, "I love you," at the same time he whispers, "I'm Patrick Lawrence."

The name jars something in her memory, leading to a moment of confusion which eclipses her elation of finally professing her feelings and expecting to hear the same in return. As the instructor yells at her to jump, the name clicks. Their eyes briefly meet, his ones of sorrow, hers, of horror. Then he's gone from view as her stomach, and heart, are left behind in her free fall.

Chapter Twenty-One: Patrick's Two Truths and a Lie

She's going to kill me. She said, "I love you," and I told her who I was. She gave me her heart, and I broke it in front of her. Maybe I'll just not open the parachute and die that way. This last is just a barely wishful thought. The free fall doesn't last nearly long enough. *Maybe I should have chosen a better time to tell her. Maybe now wasn't the best time. I should have known she would say that.*

He can see her parachute opening below him. *Good, at least she didn't want to kill herself. No, it was him she would want to kill. THINK! You need to have an action plan for when you land!* He pulls his own chute, watching her glide down to the ground, completely incapable of coming up with what to say once he lands. He watches her land and knows she's unbuckling the harness. He glides down near her, making a clean landing himself. Patrick unbuckles his harness and steps out, before turning in her direction. She's just standing there, tears falling down her face. He takes a step towards her, and she takes a step back. Patrick stops, feeling as if she had slapped him.

"How could you?" She whispers. "How could you!?!" she screams in a strangled cry. Her face contorts, whether from crying or anger, Patrick is not sure. He freezes. He had not prepared what to say and now he has nothing to answer her as he watches this woman fall apart because of him.

"How could you not tell me?!?" She's still screaming and crying, now trying to brush the tears off her face. Mickie takes a shuttering, deep breath. "Explain yourself." That fake calm is enough to knock Patrick out of his stupor.

"OK," he begins, putting his hands up in front of him, "I'll try." He also takes a labored deep breath, then begins the tale. "When I came to your house that first day, I was planning on talking to Michelle Brenner. I was going to introduce myself, tell her how sorry I was for the accident, and then move on. I had no idea you were Michelle Brenner. You were Mickie; the girl I had shared a fun time with the night before. When you opened the door, I panicked. I told the first lie that came to mind because I wasn't prepared to actually know who Michelle Brenner was."

"Why did you introduce yourself as Paul at Applebee's, if you didn't know who I was?" Mickie interrupts, glaring.

"I had just legally changed my name to Paul, earlier that day. You see, ten years after parole, you can legally change your name, and it had been ten years to the day," Patrick stammers.

"Yeah, twenty-five years to the day since you killed Ben," Mickie lashes out.

"I know. I honestly had no idea who you were, or I probably would have never sat down with you but just left the restaurant." Paul stops, unsure if he had just made matters worse, but Mickie says nothing; arms crossed and still glaring, tears still trickle from the corners of her eyes. "So, um, that first day. Yeah, I just panicked. I was shocked and lied. Then I didn't know how to recover."

"Why did you come back and ask me out?" Mickie interrupts again.

"I don't know!" Patrick is sweating, running his hands through his thinning hair. "I just felt this connection and draw towards you. Tom told me to just go over and tell you, but instead I asked you out. I felt this… strange connection and I wasn't ready to just let it go. I wanted to know why I felt this pull towards you."

"You mean besides the fact we had a shared history that you were keeping secret from me?"

"Yeah," Patrick hangs his head. "Besides that little tidbit." He looks back up at her and thinks he almost sees her mouth quiver towards a smile, but it's over in an instant and she's back to glaring at him. "So, um, after our date, I kept thinking about how upset you were over being vanilla." Mickie flushes. "And I think to myself," Patrick continues, "that I can help you get over that. So, I started planning these dates based on the Never Have I Ever card on Google." Patrick stops talking and looks at Mickie, waiting to see if she has anything to say.

"So, during these past two months, have you just been buttering me up so that when you tell me you killed my husband, I'll be nicer to you?"

"No!" Patrick assures her, taking another step forward. This time, Mickie stays put, though she still has her arms crossed and her face impassive. "These two months have been the best two months of my life... besides the fact I was keeping a secret from you." He takes another step towards her, now halfway to her.

"How could you kiss me and not tell me? How could you let this deepen and not tell me?!?" The tears start falling again, and Mickie does nothing to stop them. "Oh my gosh!" Her hands fly to her mouth. "We had sex!" Her hands go to her stomach, like she's about to be sick. "Oh my gosh," she gasps, bending over slightly and going white. "I told you I loved you – and you killed Ben!" She straightens back up and looks at him, horrified.

Patrick has filled the distance between them now and looks back at her, clearly heartbroken. "I love you, too," he whispers, voice cracking. Mickie just stares at him horror-stricken, then bends down to pick up her chute and harness.

"I never want to see or hear from you again," she whispers, not looking at him. Then she turns and jogs back to the runway.

Patrick watches her walk away, then turns around to get his stuff, unaware that tears now grace his cheeks, too.

Chapter Twenty-Two: Mickie's Labor Day

"I don't understand," Karen iterates for the thousandth time, "What happened?" She helps Mickie carry the potato salad and condiments outside. "You guys were so perfect together. You were in love!"

"Don't say that!" Mickie turns to her friend. "Look, I told you. I found out he was keeping a dark secret from me, and I can't be with a guy who keeps secrets." Mickie places the potato salad on the table and starts taking condiments from Karen.

"What secret could be so bad? I thought you really liked this guy!"

"I thought so too, but a liar once will lie again."

"OK, then tell me the big, juicy secret." Karen leans forward.

"No," Mickie retorts.

"Oh, come on. You said you're never going to see him again. We had not seen him before this summer, so the likelihood is we won't see him again. Tell me what could be so bad that you'd break off the best relationship you've ever had."

"What about Ben?"

Karen looks at Mickie a little consolingly. "Mickie, I loved you and Ben. You were sappy high school sweethearts. But you never shone like you did this summer. You've become more confident, more free... more fun, for sure." Karen gives a playful nudge. "You sure you can't forgive him?"

"Positive." Mickie turns away.

"Well, I think you should reconsider!" Karen calls after her, then goes back into the air conditioning.

"What should you reconsider, mom?" Jacob comes up next to Mickie.

"Oh, nothing." Mickie won't meet his gaze. The truth is, she does think about reconsidering. She misses Paul – no Patrick – like crazy. She has cried every day since she left him. Just talking about him now makes her chest constrict and tears well.

"Getting back with Paul?" Jacob guesses.

"Will everyone just leave me alone?" Mickie chokes out.

"Mom, if it's bothering you this much, you should tell someone." Jacob places his hand on her shoulder and gives her a one-armed hug. This is too much for Mickie, who quickly squeezes back, then turns out from his hold.

"I'm fine," she reiterates. "Let's talk about you and Mara."

Jacob watches his mom but realizes he's not going to break through. "OK…" Jacob begins slowly, then pauses.

Mickie turns to look at her son. "What is it?" she asks sharply.

"I'm going to ask Mara to marry me," Jacob quickly replies.

"Oh, Jacob! That's wonderful! I'm so excited for you!" Mickie grabs her son for a full hug. "I knew it probably would happen soon, but still… oh, I'm so happy for you guys!" She gives him another hug.

"What's all the commotion over here?" Mara asks, coming up behind Mickie.

"Oh, no commotion at all," Mickie responds, though her face betrays her glee.

"He told you, didn't he?" Mara smiles shyly.

"YES!" Mickie embraces her soon to be daughter-in-law. "And I'm so happy for the two of you! When is the date?"

"Well, we don't know for sure, yet, but probably sometime in May," Mara says, looking at Jacob. Jacob, meanwhile, is gesturing at Mara to stop talking. She looks at him confused, but Mickie misses the exchange.

"Wow! Spring! So soon?"

"What –" begins Mara, but Jacob cuts in, "Mom, it's not what you think."

Mickie turns to look at Jacob, confused. "What do mean?"

"Yeah, what do you mean?" Mara asks.

Jacob takes a deep breath, rubbing above his left eye. "Mara's pregnant."

"What?" Mickie steps back, blinking and shaking her head.

"I'm confused, what were you congratulating me for?" Mara asks, looking from Mickie to Jacob.

"This," and Jacob takes a little box out of his pocket and kneels on the ground.

"Oh my gosh!" Mara raises her hands to her mouth.

"Mara Kenan," Jacob opens the box to reveal a beautiful diamond ring, "will you marry me?"

"Oh my gosh," Mickie whispers, though no one hears her over Mara's squeal.

"Jacob! Jacob, are you sure? This is not just because of the baby?" Mara asks quickly.

"Baby?" Karen whispers in Mickie's ear. Mickie just numbly nods.

"No, Mara. I bought this before I found out you were pregnant… we were pregnant," he amends, smiling at her. "I've known for a while now that you were the woman I wanted to spend the rest of my life with. Now, what do you say?" he asks, playfully.

"Yes!" Mara responds, kneeling next to him and kissing him. "A thousand times yes!"

"I need a drink," Mickie says, turning to the house. Karen follows her.

"You know, I never have a problem with having a drink, but are you sure you want to end your prohibition this way?" Karen jokes.

"Karen, you know jolly well I didn't mean alcohol. And you won't find any here," she adds, gruffly.

Karen raises her eyebrows at her. "What's wrong with you? I thought you liked Mara. And didn't you tell me the other day you thought he would be proposing soon?"

"I do like her. And yes, I did say that. But the whole thing... You got to admit, it's a bit of a shock!" The two friends lean on opposite ends of the counter, facing each other. Mickie drinks water as Karen picks up a can of Cola.

"What's so shocking?" Karen asks. "You didn't know they were sleeping together?"

"Oh, ew, Karen, that's my son!" Mickie shudders.

"And he's happy! Why aren't you happy for him?"

"I don't know. I'm just shocked. This is all so fast."

"Did you think maybe Paul would be the one proposing this Labor Day instead of Jacob?" Karen asks gently.

"What?" Mickie gasps. "No! I mean... we were not... why would... no!"

"Are you upset because you thought you had found someone who would propose one day?"

"Karen! I'm not upset. Just shocked. See?" Mickie forces a smile. "Let's go out and congratulate them." Mickie straightens up and sways slightly, closing her eyes.

"Mickie? Oh my gosh! What's wrong? Are you OK? Do you need to sit down?" Karen is over with a hand on Mickie's shoulder in an instant.

"I'm fine," Mickie replies, opening her eyes. "Just straightened up too quickly, I think. Besides," she adds in a hushed undertone, pushing Karen's hand off, "it's probably just hormonal. I think I'm starting perimenopause."

"What? Why do you think that?"

"Well, my period's late and I've been feeling lightheaded and nauseous. Now come on, let's go back outside." Mickie leads the way, then stumbles down the steps.

"Mom! Are you OK?" Jacob and Mara rush over. Mickie sinks to the ground, clutching Karen's arm. "Yeah, yeah, I'm just," she pauses as she sits on the grass, "a little dizzy is all."

"Mom, you can't keep your eyes open – what's wrong?"

"I'm going to call an ambulance."

"No! No! Don't!" Mickie tries to stand and falls over.

"Mickie?"

"Mom?"

Mickie lies there, unconscious.

Chapter Twenty-Three: Patrick's Blast from the Past

You can tell when you enter Grant Point; it's one thing entering Neilsor after leaving Hadad, but Grant Point is something else entirely. Everything is dark, dank, and rundown. There is no differentiation between any of the apartment buildings, no characterization to the individual apartments. Little grass, and the little there is browning. Cracked asphalt and sidewalks. There are no toys or bikes outside because someone would steal them. Huddles of gangs group around certain key points: the old Thoreau building, the liquor store, the gas station with only one working pump. If you do see kids out, like today with it being a holiday, they are always in groups. You never hang out alone.

Patrick chose to park his truck at Gaither's and walk the mile into Grant Point, because he thought it would be safer for his truck. Even though he used to live here, he had not been back since that fateful night over twenty-five years ago. No one would recognize him. He didn't even know if anyone he knew still lived here.

Patrick had had no contact with friends or family since going to jail. No one came to visit, send a card, or drop a line. When he got out, he was bitter and knew going back to his old life would tempt him to go back to unhealthy habits, so he had stayed away. Over time, he had just gotten used to not thinking about this place or these people. They had shut him out of their lives, and he had closed that door forever.

Or so he had thought. Yet here he was. He still wasn't entirely sure why he chose to come to his childhood home this Labor Day. Maybe he thought if he could reconcile his childhood, he could fix things with Mickie. He wasn't sure. Regardless, he was here. Heading towards Apartment 10B.

"Hey, you there." Patrick turns to see four younger guys walking towards him.

"Hey," Patrick replies slowly.

"We don't need no more low life's. Whatcha doin' walking by yourself down here?" The speaker was in his upper-20s, and clearly the gang leader.

"I'm looking for my old home. Does the Lawrence family still live in Apartment 10B?" Patrick keeps his tone and gaze level, knowing that to make any sort of move would pull the weapons from these guys.

The men shift and the leader quirks an eyebrow up. "You a Lawrence?"

"Yes. Patrick Lawrence. Omar, Nicky, Majesty, and Ace are my younger siblings." The guys clearly know at least one of his siblings, hopefully on good terms.

The leader huffs. One of the men leans forward and whispers, "I heard he went to jail for killing a cracker." Patrick grimaces. The leader sees and says, "Don't be feeling guilty. It's the gutter or slammer for most here. Yeah, the Lawrence's still live in 10B. What's left of 'em. Come on, guys." The leader jerks his head in dismissal then turns around. Patrick nods back and waits until they all turn before walking the rest of the way.

He knocks on the door of 10B and waits until a little girl peaks through the curtain. She opens the door a crack and Patrick says, "Hey, I'm probably your uncle Patrick. Um... is your mum or dad home?" She closes the door, then a moment later, a man opens it grinning.

"Patrick! My gosh, it is you! I thought you were dead!"

Patrick grins, shyly. "Nicky?"

"It's Nick, now," the younger man replies, still grinning. "Come in, come in. Mum's in the kitchen. Go say hi and I'll round up the hooligans."

Patrick walks into the familiar living room, sees the girl who had opened the door sitting on the edge of the same couch he used to sit on. Nick waves him on through to the kitchen, while he goes up the stairs, calling out names. Patrick walks through the living room into the kitchen and stops. A woman with saggy, leathery skin sits at the table, trying to get a needle into her arm.

"There you are, Nick. Help your momma out." She looks up and frowns. "Who are you?"

"It's me, momma. It's Patrick."

"Patrick!" she raises her eyebrows then squints at him. "Last I heard, you was getting out of jail. But you never showed up." She glares at him. Patrick feels like the weight of the world is settling on him. The lady harrumphs. "Never mind that. You're here now. Help me get this in."

"No, mum."

She glares back up at him. "What'dju say?"

"Momma…"

"Don't 'momma' me. I didn't raise no namby pamby wussie boy." She looks down at her arm and readjusts the needle. It slides in this time, and she sighs. Then she glares back up at Patrick. "Whatcha doin' here?"

"I just came to see you."

"Why? I ain't got no money for you."

"Just to see you."

"Well, you saw me. You gonna move back in?"

"No, mum." Patrick feels dead inside. This woman had not missed him at all. There was no warm welcome, hugs, or anything but disgust.

"Then git on out. I ain't got nuff food for Nick's brats, let alone an ungrateful whelp." She pulls some pill boxes towards her, and Patrick walks out.

Nick is waiting for him in the living room, along with four children aged toddler to about ten.

"Kids, this is your Uncle Patrick. Pat, this is Marci, Louise, Mac, and Evan." The kids all wave at him, Evan with one thumb in his mouth. "OK, go on back upstairs and play." Once the kids are upstairs, Nick asks Patrick, "So, what did you think of the saggy, baggy elephant?"

"Nick, why didn't you warn me?"

"What?"

"She was shooting up dope!"

"Yeah, what else is new? She's always done drugs."

"But your kids...!"

"Yeah, I don't like it, but I don't get them all the time and I try to keep them upstairs if she's shooting up. I about lost it on her when I caught her using Louise to help. She's nasty, but seeing as I'm the only one she's got, she doesn't get too mean."

Patrick just shakes his head. "What happened to everyone else?"

"Well, Omar died in a gang shooting soon after you went to jail. Majesty, the whore, slept with everyone here then found a sucker to take her to Ohio. My guess is she just used him to get out; never heard from her after she left. Ace was killed in a domestic shooting about five years ago; apparently his girlfriend was cheating on another guy with him."

Patrick drops his head into his hands. He raises it back up and chokes out, "Dad?"

"That loser jumped ship and ran. Moved to Texas, I heard. This was after Omar. Someone called the police on Mum about drugs again and there was still us three teenagers. Dad didn't want the responsibility so left one day for work and never came back."

Patrick's shoulders slump. "Nick... I'm sorry. I should have come back sooner."

"Don't worry, Bruh. What about you? What happened after jail?"

Patrick hesitates, not sure what to share. "Well, I had to be on parole. I got a job at the factory –"

"You got a place?" Nick interrupts.

Patrick hesitates, then nods.

Nick nods back, then motions for Patrick to continue.

"I got an apartment and finally another truck."

"Cool, man."

"I really should have checked in before now," Patrick says again.

Nick shakes his head. "Look, you found a way out. You got jail time but then made something of yourself. You didn't want to get stuck here. I get it. I'm just glad you came back."

"I'm not staying, Nick."

"No, I know. But you came back. Better than Majesty or dad."

"Why do you stay?"

Nick contemplates this thought. "I guess cuz it's home."

"But you seem like you turned out OK. Why stay and risk your children with mum's lifestyle?"

"Who else would take care of her? Besides, I only get visitation. Four kids, three different women. Didn't marry any of 'em. I'm a simple guy. This supplies a simple life. A life I'm used to."

Patrick shakes his head and stands up. "I'm heading out."

Nick nods his head and stands up, too. He walks Patrick to the door and holds out his hand. Patrick shakes it and looks at his brother. Patrick's eyes are sad, Nick's accepting. Patrick takes his phone out and opens his contacts.

"Can I add you? We can chat some more. Or you could bring the kids, or whichever ones you have, and visit me sometime?"

"Sure." They exchange numbers and Patrick heads out. Before he puts his phone back in his pocket, it starts to vibrate. The screen reads "Mickie." Patrick almost drops it! He catches it, then looks for a place to stop and answer it. He finds a dip in a rundown stone fence and sits on that before taking a deep breath and answering it. "Hello?"

Chapter Twenty-Four: Mickie's Surprise

Mickie had only passed out momentarily. She was up before the ambulance got there and had protested having to use them. She had protested all the treatment so far. She had had to undergo a urinalysis, stress test, EKG, and blood draw. Currently, she was hooked to a machine watching her heart rate and oxygen levels. She felt silly. People passed out all the time. Sure, she may need to increase vitamins or something, but she was sure she was fine, and she kept telling everyone this.

"I just want to go home. We left the food out – it will be all wasted by now. Let's just grab a couple pizzas and relax."

"It's not OK to pass out, mom. We just want to make sure everything is fine. Is there anything you can think of that you haven't told the doctors or nurses yet?" Jacob was holding Mickie's hand, gazing worriedly at her.

"I told you, I'm fine. I told them everything. This is really more embarrassing with you here. It's probably menopausal."

"You're my mom. I don't care what it is – I want to make sure you're OK."

"And Mickie, I made sure to clear everything up before we left. I put all the food away after you came around and before the ambulance arrived. So don't worry about the food waste," Mara adds, coming up to stand beside Jacob at Mickie's side.

"Kids, this is silly. The EKG and stress test came back fine. We're just waiting for the results of the other tests and then I'll be released. Go home. Enjoy the remainder of the day." Mickie puts her other hand on top of Jacob's.

"I'll stay and make sure she gets home OK, if you guys want to go get some food. Mickie's right, she will be released here soon enough," pipes up Karen from a chair at the foot of the bed. She eyes Mickie with a curious expression.

"I'm not leaving. But we could go down to the food court. Karen, please call if they come back." Jacob lets go of Mickie's hand and grabs Mara's. They walk swiftly through the curtain and are out of sight.

"Karen, you can go, too. I can let you all know what they say if they get in before you all are back. You must be starving," Mickie says, looking over at her best friend.

"Oh no. I'm not leaving here for anything. I have a question for you," Karen replies, rising from the chair and walking towards the head of the bed.

Mickie raises her eyebrows, "What?"

"Did you and Paul have sex?"

"What?!?" Mickie gasps, bringing one hand to her chest.

"Did you guys have sex?"

"Why on earth are you asking me that now?" Mickie hisses, looking at the curtain.

"Because, bestie," Karen says, drawing out the word, "there is another possible explanation to all of this." She lets that hang in the air.

Mickie starts laughing. "Karen, I'm forty-three years old. I haven't had sex in close to a decade. I'm pretty sure that ship has sailed." Mickie shakes her head, but Karen places her hands on her hips.

"So, you and Paul never..."

Mickie hesitates and Karen seizes it.

"You did!"

"Sh!" Mickie hushes frantically. "Just once, a few weeks ago."

"A few weeks?!? Why didn't you tell me?!?" Karen hisses back, leaning towards Mickie.

"Because... I don't know. It was on an impulse. And it felt special. And I didn't know how to just go about letting you know. I mean, that seems weird."

"Not really. This is huge!" Karen pauses then asks, "That's not why you broke up, is it? Was he that bad in bed?"

"Oh, Karen! No! And we were not in bed," Mickie adds sheepishly.

Karen's eyes widen.

"I took him skinny dipping." Mickie explains, quietly.

Karen's jaw drops. "Wow. I didn't know you had that in you." Karen pauses, thinking all this through. "So, you finally initiated a date, you had amazing sex, then you went skydiving and broke up? What happened?!?"

Luckily, a nurse saves Mickie from having to answer by coming through the curtain. "Good afternoon, Michelle. I have the results of your lab work and there is something we need to discuss. Do you want to do this privately?"

"Hell no," Karen answers. The nurse shoots her a reproving glance. Karen just shrugs.

"No, I'm fine, you can share them in front of her," Mickie replies, shaking her head at Karen.

"You're pregnant."

"I knew it!" Karen exclaims.

"What?!?" Apparently, Jacob and Mara had just come back from the food court.

Mickie just lies motionless, looking from the nurse to Jacob, and back to the nurse, wide eyed. "Are you sure?"

"Positive."

"Sometimes there are false positives," Mickie reminds her, beginning to tremble.

"Both urine and blood work say the same thing. You're pregnant," the nurse replies, gently. "Now there are options –"

"WAIT!" Mickie interrupts, sitting forward. "I don't want to abort. I'm just in shock. I'm forty-three. I should not be having a baby. My son is having a baby! I just need a few minutes to process."

The nurse nods and walks around Jacob and Mara and out past the curtain, closing it shut behind her.

Jacob stares at Mickie, aghast. "How did this happen?"

"I'm not getting into specifics with you," Mickie retorts, a little color coming back to her cheeks.

"Is it Paul?"

"Yes, of course, it's Paul. Who else would it be?"

"Well, I didn't know it was possible, so excuse me for clarifying," Jacob growls back.

Mickie reels on him. "Look, this is shocking to all of us. Paul and I did it once about a month ago. I didn't think to tell anyone because it's nobody's business. I didn't think anything would happen – we're in our forties! But I need to process here." Mickie massages her temples. She looks back at Jacob and Mara, apologetically. "This doesn't take away from you guys," she pauses before adding, "I'm sorry."

Mara bracingly laughs. "Well, at least they'll have each other growing up. There was no hope of other kids for this one for a while." Mara looks down at her belly, rubbing it.

"Hopefully yours is at least older," Jacob replies, with a shaky smile.

Mickie looks at them both and starts to cry. They all hug and Karen slowly claps. They all turn to look at her.

"Now all we need is to fix you and Paul back up," Karen says, then barks a laugh. "Man, won't he be shocked!" Karen continues laughing.

"Mom…" Jacob leans back a little from Mickie but holds her hand and looks deeply into her eyes. "Whatever the reason for breaking it off… does this change things for you?"

"I don't know..." Mickie whispers. "I guess I have to tell him. I don't know if he will want to be a part of this baby's life or not. I guess that's where I'll need to start."

"Mom," Jacob says forcefully. "You don't have to tell him anything. If you can't forgive him, then leave him behind. But if you're thinking about forgiving him for whatever happened, then yes, you will have to tell him. And then, his response will decide things. But you choose if you want him to even have that choice."

Mickie gazes at Jacob, then squeezes his hand. "I think I want to tell him."

"Are you sure?"

"Yes," and this time Mickie really smiles, a watery smile that leads to tears falling down her face. She turns her head away and tries to shield her face from everyone. "I miss him so much. Maybe... maybe this is God's way of forcing me to give him another chance... and to fully let go of Ben."

"Oh, mom." Jacob leans in.

"Mickie." Karen leans in.

Jacob gets up and pulls out a phone. He texts a quick message then puts it down on the table. He steps back to Mara and puts his arm around her. She smiles up at him, giving him a squeeze. "Karen," Jacob says, "would you come get some food, please?" Mickie and Karen both sharply look up at the two mischievous faces.

"Why would I do that?" Karen retorts.

"Probably so I can have a few minutes alone with Mickie," says a soft, male voice from behind the curtain.

Chapter Twenty-Five: Patrick Gets Another Second Chance

Mickie gasps and blushes; Karen's jaw drops.

"How did you – " Mickie begins but doesn't finish. "How long have you – " but again, Mickie can't finish the sentence.

"I called him and told him you were in the hospital," Jacob explains.

Mickie turns to her son, "How? When?" Then she adds, quieter, "Why?" Patrick's expression saddens, but he stays where he is.

"I took your phone and called him once we got here. I asked if he really cared about you and listened to him. I told him you were in the hospital, and he could come but he could not see you until I had figured out if you wanted to see him. He got here while Mara and I were downstairs. I had him stay out in the waiting room and just now texted him that you were ready to see him. He knows nothing besides you're here." Jacob says this last sentence pointedly, sending his mom a message that Patrick doesn't understand, but isn't going to push right now.

"Could I have a few minutes alone with Mickie, please?" Patrick asks the room at large, but he looks at Mickie.

Mickie meets his gaze, and everyone can tell they are sizing the other up. No one moves until Mickie nods her head and says, "Yes, a few minutes alone would be nice." She looks at Karen when she says "alone," and smiles, slightly, once she finishes, letting everyone know she's OK and wants this.

Jacob and Mara walk out together, Jacob clapping Patrick on the shoulder as he passes. Karen hugs Mickie and whispers something in her ear, which causes Mickie to push her teasingly. Then Karen, too, walks out, smirking at Patrick as she passes and whispering loudly, "Don't mess this one up."

Patrick watches them round the corner, then steps forward, closing the curtain all the way. "Are you OK?" he asks, brows furrowed at the sight of her hooked to a machine.

Mickie glances at him, blushes, and nods. "Yeah, I'm fine."

"You didn't tell Jacob about me." Patrick says it as a statement, but there is a question in his eyes.

"I didn't even tell Karen." Mickie meets his eyes and then looks away. "I don't really know why. Maybe because if I did, I was afraid they would make my choice for me."

"What choice?" Patrick asks, softly, taking another step closer.

"Whether to talk to or see you again," Mickie responds, just as softly and still not meeting his eyes.

Patrick steps up to the bed and places one hand under Mickie's chin, gently tilting it to look at him. "I'm so sorry," he chokes out, tears welling behind his eyes. He keeps his gaze fixed on hers and adds, "I should have told you from the beginning. I was just afraid that I would not have a say in seeing or talking to you. I was afraid you would shut me out forever. That doesn't excuse how I handled things," he hurriedly adds, "but I think you now can relate to that."

Mickie nods, though barely, her eyes also fixed on his.

"I thought I lost you. I wanted so badly to fix it, but I thought I needed to respect your wishes. I was scared. But I was even more scared today when Jacob called. Mickie, I know it may be too late and it may not be the right time, but I love you. I love you fiercely. I'll do anything to stay with you. Even if you don't want to go out anymore, please, let me stay in your life. I want to make things up to you." Patrick pauses and adds, "Today, I went to see my family for the first time since the accident," and he finally drops his hand from her chin.

Mickie swallows, hard, and asks, "you haven't been home in twenty-five years?"

Patrick gives a short, hollow laugh. "I haven't seen any family or friends in twenty-five years. Everyone in my life now has been in my life since the accident."

Mickie just stares at him.

"You can't even understand my decision, can you?" Patrick asks.

Mickie shakes her head.

"I was so hurt and angry that no one came to see me in jail, that I refused to go see them once I got out. I only officially changed my name this summer, but I have been going by Paul for a while now. I wasn't trying to run from my record – I was trying to forget my past because it hurt so much to think about. I was a mess before the accident. Talking to my brother today, I realized how lucky I was to have been in prison. My other two brothers are dead, and no one knows about my dad or sister. My mother is still shooting up drugs and is barely a shell of a human. Even Nicky, four kids with three women, and still living with mom and supporting her," Patrick stops, breathing hard. Mickie just looks on, a little horrified, but also softening.

"Paul... Patrick... I'm sorry. I honestly can't imagine what that was like to grow up in, or even to have spent the last twenty-five years as. I guess it makes sense you lied." Patrick grimaces, but Mickie reaches out and lays her hand on his arm. "You did lie. By withholding the truth, you lied. But I understand now." Mickie stops and looks at Patrick, he meets her gaze. "The question now, is, what do you want? Do you want to keep running?"

Patrick locks eyes with her and says, unblinkingly, "I want to be with you."

Mickie starts to smile and Patrick's tension eases. "Do you want to know what I'm in here for?"

Patrick leans back a little, shocked at this change of topic. "Yeah?"

Mickie smiles and bites her lip before saying, "I'm pregnant."

Patrick's eyes grow wide. "You're pregnant?"

Mickie nods and adds, "Technically, we're pregnant," she says, emphasizing the "we're."

Patrick stares, then grins and hugs her. He pulls back, looks in her eyes, then kisses her. "Was that OK?" he asks, looking at her face.

She smiles and leans forward, "I told you I was having our baby. I think it's OK if you kiss me."

Patrick grabs her face and kisses her again.

"Hey, can we come in?" Jacob calls from behind the curtain.

Patrick pulls away and Mickie responds, "You can come in."

Jacob, Mara, and Karen come in, looking from Patrick to Mickie. "I take it, you guys made up?" Jacob asks.

Patrick grins at him, resting his hand on Jacob's shoulder. "What do you want, a brother or sister?"

The whole room laughs. The nurse comes back in and hands Mickie the paperwork, letting her know she's free to leave and when to make a follow-up appointment. Everyone files out while Mickie dresses. When she opens the curtain, only Patrick is still there.

"The others went back to the house to start dinner. They asked if I could give you a ride home."

"How sweet of them," Mickie responds sarcastically. They hold hands as they start walking.

"I was thinking, how should I tell them?"

"Tell them what?" Mickie asks.

"Tell them the truth about who I am."

Mickie stops in her tracks, forcing Patrick to turn around. "Why would you tell them?" she asks, a little scared.

Patrick smiles sadly and steps towards her. He puts his hands around her arms and gazes at her, lovingly. "I don't want to live a lie around them forever. I want them to be my family, too. And families should not lie to one another, don't you think?"

Mickie blinks, then stands on her tiptoes to kiss him. "I'll help you figure out what to say." Mickie pauses then continues, "And when to say it," she says with a smile.

Patrick softly laughs and kisses her nose, then her mouth. "I'll follow your lead, wherever you go." They kiss again, then walk out of the hospital together.

Chapter Twenty-Six: Paul's New Life

December 31, 2022

Paul sits in the little church library reminiscing about the past few months. Mickie and he stayed up all night Labor Day making plans. First, what to do about them having a baby. Paul had told Mickie that he was a Christian and believed the right thing to do was to get married. Mickie was slightly hesitant at first, bringing up the fact they had only been going out a short bit, had just got back together, and their history.

"Do you see yourself married to me at some point?" Patrick asks Mickie.

"Yes, I guess. I mean… yes, I do. I guess when I see us with this baby, I see us together, and I guess that would imply married," Mickie works out.

"Then let's get married. I'll ask Pastor Ted if he'll do the ceremony, if you don't mind."

Pastor Ted was delighted to perform the ceremony, but under two conditions: they had to go through premarital counseling with him and they had to refrain from living/sleeping together. Through premarital counseling and talks with Paul, it wasn't long before Pastor Ted also baptized Mickie.

Mickie had always dreamed of a winter wedding, and neither of them wanted a long engagement. They chose New Year's Eve, seeing it as an ironically fitting date for starting their new life together.

The second thing they had discussed was who and when to tell the truth. They decided the only people who needed to know were Karen, Jacob, and Mara. Tom and Pastor Ted already knew and no one else in their lives needed to know.

They told Karen first, Mickie believing she would take it the easiest. Sure enough, Karen took it in stride. She was a little shocked and wanted all the details but accepted it right away.

"That explains the draw you felt to him! You knew," she put air quotes around the word, "each other from before, but really had no interaction to recognize each other. But your hearts felt the connection and called to each other! It's like, you were two halves of a broken heart, and the hearts knew it, but the minds didn't!" Karen got more animated as she talked, like she was having an epiphany; by the end of her speech, she was halfway out of her seat.

Paul and Mickie look at each other and smile. They had talked about that draw as well.

"I'm not sure I would put it that way," Mickie begins. "That kind of takes what Ben and I had out of the picture."

Karen falls back against the chair, gaping at Mickie. "You talk about Ben that way in front of him?!?" Karen turns to Paul. "And you're OK with that?!?"

Paul takes Mickie's hand and squeezes it.

"Ben was a part of both of our lives, for good," Mickie says.

"And bad," Paul finishes. "We see it more like this: that accident connected our hearts by an invisible string. Neither of us had healed from that accident, though in different fashions. Mickie's heart was still broken, even twenty-five years later. And mine... well, it was like it had a cut that would not heal. Every time I'd think I was over it; something would come up; like a cut that scabs, but then reopens."

"How lovely," Karen replies, sarcastically.

They told Jacob and Mara together, the next time they visited. Mara kept silent but her eyes grew like a ripple in a pond. Jacob, also, was silent as they explained, but they could see him clenching Mara's hand. Once they finished, they waited several long moments before Jacob spoke.

"I knew there was something off. I knew you were hiding a secret." Jacob says both statements matter-of-factly, but there is a little heat behind them.

"I know," Mickie says, also clenching Paul's hand.

"And I knew you suspected something," Paul replies, squeezing Mickie's hand in reassurance, even though he feels just as worried.

"Why didn't you tell me after you left him?" Jacob asks his mom.

Mickie's eyes brim with tears, "I was scared," she trembles, clenching Paul's hand even tighter. "I knew I was in love with him but was also so hurt. I could not decide if I would forgive him or not. And if I did but told you the truth… I feared how you would react. I was having such a tough time with the thought of losing Paul. I couldn't fathom how you would forgive him if I returned to him." Mickie's tears fall down her cheeks, but she keeps her hand in Paul's.

"You're with him now and telling me. What does that mean?" Jacob asks.

"It means," Mickie takes a shaky breath, "that I'm choosing to forgive him and spend the rest of my life with him."

Jacob stares at the two of them, then shakes his head downward, running his left hand through his hair. When he looks back up, he has a twisted smile on his face. "First we're having babies at the same time and now this? Please don't tell Karen or we may end up on Oprah."

They all let out shaky laughs, the tension easing in the room.

"So," Jacob gets serious again. "Are you Patrick or Paul?"

"Paul," Paul replies.

That had been another topic of conversation that first night. Patrick had legally changed his name to Paul that summer, but, as Tom liked to remind him, he was still Patrick Lawrence. They talked about this one for hours that first night. Was it living a lie to remain Paul? Was Patrick his true self and Paul the name under which he was hiding? They decided that Paul was really who he had become in prison. Patrick had chosen the name Paul, because of the story in the Bible: how the man Saul, after his conversion, changed his name to Paul. Patrick, after converting, was a new man. And even though he had not been able to legally change his name, he was a different man.

"Paul is who your family know me as. Patrick is who they associate with Ben. I'm not that guy anymore," Paul had explained to Mickie.

Paul now gets up as Tom and Jacob enter the church library.

"Happy wedding day," Tom says, shaking his hand.

"How are you feeling?" Jacob asks, giving Paul a one-armed hug.

"Great," Paul replies, smiling at them. "How's Mara today?"

"Sick as a dog this morning, but luckily her morning sickness seems to be just in the morning. How's mom?" Jacob asks, leaning against a bookshelf with his hands in his pockets.

"She said she was fine; we've only texted briefly today. Karen spent the night and brought her over." Paul crosses the room and then walks back to the center.

"You're pacing," Jacob notes.

"I'm a little nervous – it is my wedding day," Paul feebly jokes.

"Relax." Tom claps him on the shoulder and hands him a stick of gum. "Take it; it'll help calm your nerves."

"Are you crazy?" Paul laughs. "I'll forget I have it and then have to swallow it! Thanks, but I'll pass."

Pastor Ted opens the door. "You guys ready?" They all stand up straight. "Tom. Jacob. You come with me to the foyer. Paul, when the music starts, you come out and stand on the top step, just like we practiced."

Tom and Jacob follow Pastor Ted out of the library and close the door; Paul resumes his pacing. In no time at all the music starts and Paul walks out of the library. There is about fifty people there: a handful of Mickie's coworkers, several congregants (Paul and Mickie had placed membership at Hadad Church of Christ), and Nicky and his family. Paul smiles at Nick, who gives him a thumbs up before placing his hand around Angelique's shoulders. Paul had ended up telling Nick the whole truth as well and was encouraging Nick to settle down and move to Hadad. He was having mixed results, but he is happy Nick is here.

The song changes and Jacob and Mara walk down the aisle. Paul had expected Jacob to be his best man, but Mickie wanted Karen as Maid of Honor and Jacob wanted to walk with Mara. Dropping Mara off on her side, Jacob walks to his place, stopping to shake hands with Paul. Jacob slips something into his hand, smirking, then walks to his place. Paul, confused, slips it into his pocket, thinking it's gum. Now Tom is handing Paul something while masking it as a handshake. Paul looks at the little package and almost laughs aloud. It's a condom. He slides it into his pocket and shakes his head at the two men who wear identical smirks.

Just then, the song changes and the double doors open. Mickie confidently walks down the aisle by herself, a breathtaking vision. She smiles at people as she passes but keeps glancing up at Paul. Paul must remind himself to breathe. In the last few steps it takes for her to reach him, he realizes just how much he loves this woman. Silently, he prays, "Thank you, God. Thank you for changing my life. Thank you for everything I went through to get to this moment where I know exactly where I belong." With that, he smiles, taking Mickie's hand, ready to commit himself forever to the healer of his heart.

Chapter Twenty-Seven: Mickie's New List

April 2, 2023

Today has been one of the craziest days of my life, yet I'm so happy as I write in this journal. This was a hospital gift from my husband, who wants me to get back into writing. So, a quick introduction (because that's what I do with journals).

My name is Michelle Anne Brenner, but everyone calls me Mickie. I grew up as an only child and started dating Benjamin Brenner in middle school and through high school. We got married right after graduation. Twenty-six days later, he dies in a drunk driving accident; the young man who kills him and survives goes to prison for fifteen years. I found out I'm pregnant and have a son, Jacob Benjamin Brenner. I raised him on my own.

In the twenty-five years that follow, it's mostly Jacob and I, along with my best friend, Karen. During this time, both of my parents die, and my in-laws disown us. I rarely date and never have a long-term relationship. In hindsight, I was depressed, though a doctor never diagnosed me or put me on any medications. Karen was the only reason I ever got out; Jacob was my only reason for living.

Last July, on the twenty-fifth anniversary of that fateful car crash, Karen dragged me out of the house. While out to eat, a man walks in, and I feel an immediate, unexplainable draw to him. Karen, of course, brings him over to our table. The next day, he shows up at my house! It's purely an accident, but later that afternoon, he asks me out.

On our first date, I tell him about being vanilla and how I judge my vanilla-ness on these "Never Have I Ever" cards. He goes home and sets up dates around the cards. Thus begins the best summer of my life (at forty-three; a little sad). We go to a gun range, a karaoke bar, sky diving, and I even get a tattoo (it's a tulip on my right hip)! I introduce him to Jacob and his girlfriend, Mara (Jacob doesn't like Paul from the onset).

Three days after getting the tattoo, I initiated a date and take Paul skinny dipping (he was hesitant, but it was the hottest, coolest thing I have ever done). Desire overcomes us, and we give way to lustful passions. At our next date, I tell him I love him, and he tells me he killed Ben. That destroys me. I tell him to never talk to or see me again, but it doesn't take long before my resolve starts to crack.

On Labor Day, I pass out right after Jacob 1) tells me Mara is pregnant and 2) proposes to her. After multiple tests, the nurse tells me I'm pregnant, as well (at forty-three)! Jacob, meanwhile, calls Paul and tells him I'm in the hospital; he waits to hear from Jacob to see if I have forgiven him. To cut it short, I had. I tell him I'm pregnant, and we're married on New Year's Eve.

This pregnancy has been much worse than the one with Jacob; but, with twenty-five years between them, I guess that's expected. I developed gestational diabetes early on and went into preterm labor around 32 weeks. On one of my many visits to the hospital, my blood pressure was way high, and they decided to induce me. So, earlier today, after 2 hours of labor, my son was born.

At 5:24PM, Josiah Lawrence Brenner was born at 5 pounds, 3 ounces, 19 inches long. I'm so happy he's over the five-pound mark, as that hopefully means he won't stay in the NICU long. So far, he has a little liquid in his lungs and hypoglycemia (low blood sugar), but the staff say he's doing remarkably well for how early he came. I haven't been able to see him much yet, but he's the most adorable creature on earth. He has coppery eyes, soft skin, full lips, and the bounciest curly hair you can imagine! His low blood sugar is partly from not attaching well when I have tried to breast feed him. The nurses say if he still doesn't latch at this next feeding, we'll need to switch to formula. I have already started pumping, as I want him to get as much breast milk as possible, even if it's from a bottle.

You may be wondering about the last name. When Paul and I got married, he took my last name. This way, Jacob and Josiah have the same last name; besides, Paul really didn't care (he had already legally changed his first name from Patrick to Paul, so a last name change for marriage's sake wasn't an issue for him). I can't really understand this, as I never went back to my maiden name, even though I was only married to Ben for a few weeks. But I appreciate it and strive to put myself in Paul's shoes as much as I can, as his experiences are so alien to me.

You may also be wondering why we chose Josiah. Josiah means God supports and heals. While in prison, Paul was baptized. During premarital counseling, I was baptized. We both wanted a name with God in the meaning, but we also wanted a name to do with healing. God bringing us together was a miracle. The fact that we both needed each other, when that accident had scarred us both, can only be God's doing. Patrick likes to say he helped heal my broken heart and I helped heal his bleeding heart.

Well, I'm getting tired. It's been an exceedingly long, emotional day. I'm still recovering from labor and only get little spurts of rest between nurses checking on me and bringing Josiah to me. Before I close, I want to start on a new list, since Paul helped check off most of the Never Have I Ever list. This is what I have come up with so far and I'll add to it as things come to me:

1. Write a novel (maybe after Paul and me, as it's pretty unbelievable and romantic)

2. Raise Josiah to know and love the Lord

3. Be the best grandma I can be (Mara is due in five weeks!)

4. Try new things

5. Live happily ever after with Paul

THE END

Acknowledgements

I have been writing since I was a little girl, but I have not put myself out there with my writing until last year. In 2022, I committed to being a writer and one of the first groups I joined on Facebook was Moms Who Write. It was there I met Teshelle Combs, who introduced me to Kindle Vella. Thank you Moms Who Write and Tess for jumpstarting my writing career.

Moms Who Write also helped kickstart the Southeastern Michigan Female Writers Club. Thank you to Elise, Wendy, Lindsay, and the rest of the girls for being stalwart supporters this past year and a half.

Thank you to the different Vella Facebook groups – their promos, support, encouragement, information, and connections.

Thank you to the Vella readers, especially to Lara, Angie, and Debra who read the first draft of BBH as it was being written and uploaded to KV. Thank you for sticking with me through the droughts, encouraging me to finish, leaving comments, and especially rating and reviewing it. Your need to know what happened next drove me to finally finish a draft and is the reason this is my first published long work.

Thank you to my beta readers: Mary, Elizabeth, AJ, Kerri, and Michelle. Thank you for helping to refine BBH into the best version of itself and for being so quick to read, encourage, and guide.

Thank you to Caleb, AJ, Elena, Sarah, Lara, Wendy, Elise, and Lindsay for continuing to ask about BBH throughout the whole process, providing encouragement and resources.

To all who have read, whether in part or whole, thank you. To those who have asked about it and followed my progress, thank you.

To my family, especially AJ, SJ, and Ashton – thank you for allowing me this time.

www.ingramcontent.com/pod-product-compliance
Lightning Source LLC
Chambersburg PA
CBHW061254170626
46809CB00007B/2984

* 9 7 8 1 9 5 7 7 0 7 2 4 2 *